MRS HENDERSON

by the same author

OUT OF THE WAR

MRS HENDERSON

Francis Wyndham

Moyer Bell Limited
Mt. Kisco, New York

Published by Moyer Bell Limited

Originally published in the United Kingdom as *MRS HENDERSON AND OTHER STORIES* by Jonathan Cape Ltd., London.
cover painting by Jane Human

5 4 3 2 1

LIBRARY OF CONGRESS CATALOGING IN PUBLICATION DATA

Wyndham, Francis
Mrs Henderson
Originally published: Mrs Henderson and other stories.
London: J. Cape
I. Title.

PR6073.Y67M7 1985 823'.914 86-17377

ISBN 0-918825-49-0

Manufactured in the United States of America

Contents

Acknowledgments

The title story in this collection appeared in the *London Magazine*, 'Obsessions' in the *New Review*, 'The Half Brother' and 'The Ground Hostess' in the *London Review of Books*. My thanks are due to their respective Editors: Alan Ross, Ian Hamilton and Karl Miller. I am especially grateful to Karl Miller for his encouragement during the writing of this book, and to Susannah Clapp, Assistant Editor of the *London Review of Books*, for her help and advice.

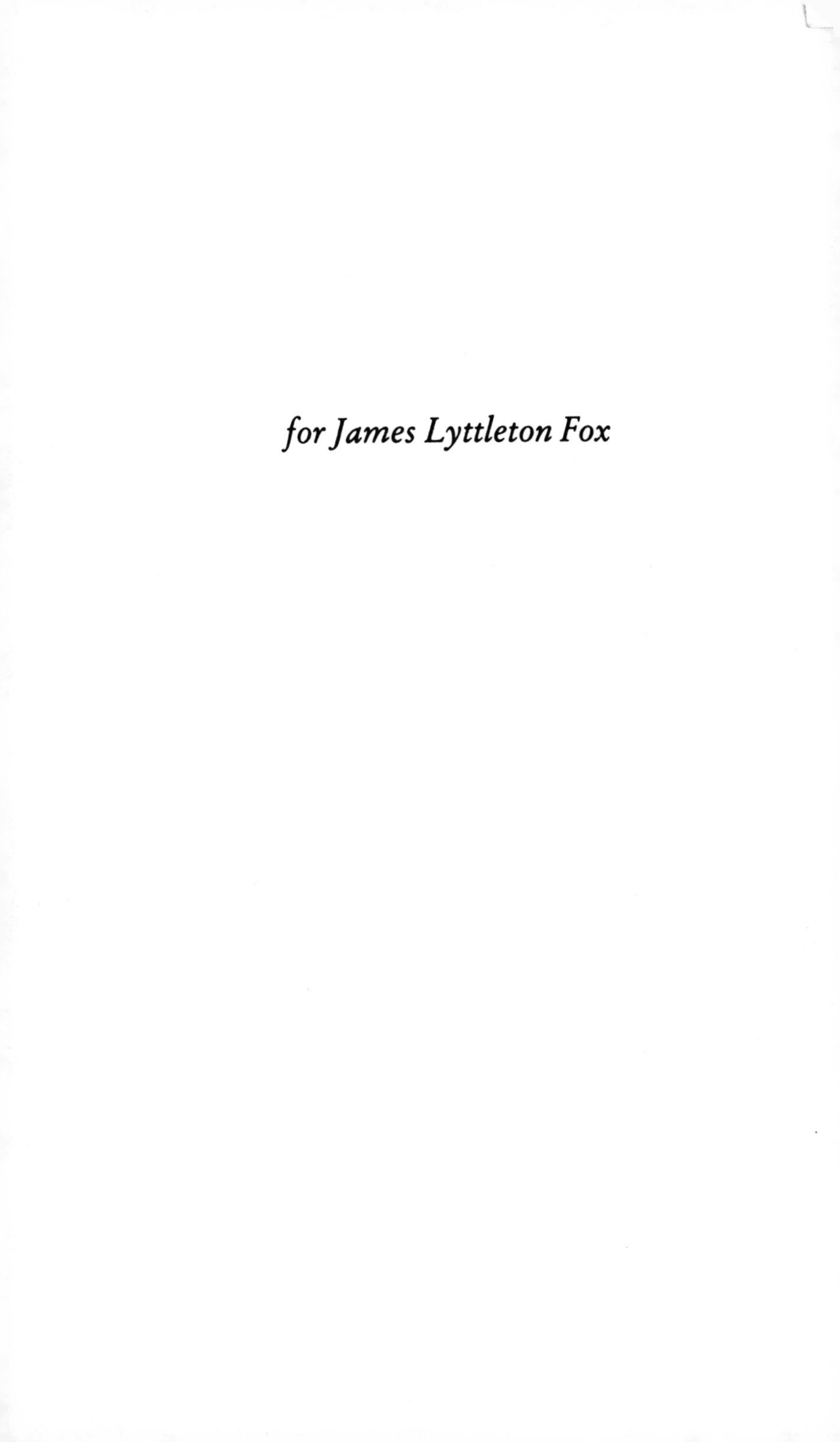

for James Lyttleton Fox

Mrs Henderson

Henderson's people lived in London. For that reason he was pitied, even despised, by most of the other boys, but to me it made him an object of envy. A snobbish assumption prevailed in this seedily conventional prep school that anything urban was somehow common; to 'live in the country' was the desired norm, while the grandest thing of all was to come from Scotland. (The school itself was situated on the outskirts of Oxford.) Henderson and I knew better. I associated London only with rare, ecstatic treats and could hardly imagine such a glamorous place being somebody's home. For his part, Henderson revealed an intimate knowledge of the Underground Railway and certain bus routes with a slightly proprietary air, as if his connection with them might be more privileged than that of a mere passenger. His father worked in the Civil Service, and Henderson had inside information about such matters as the latest designs for postage stamps and banknotes, in which he took a sober and responsible interest. I cultivated his company because I loved to hear him talk about the various monuments in Kensington Gardens and the new cinemas in Leicester Square; gratified and mildly surprised to find himself commanding any kind of audience, he tolerated mine. At the time of our friendship, we were both ten. Henderson was big for his age, with a very white skin and hair the colour of Quink.

Everybody at the school was hungry all the time. On summer nights, boys would creep in pairs from their dormitories down to the changing-room (where one window, due to some self-perpetuating oversight, could easily be opened) and out into the cool kitchen garden to eat peas fresh from the pods. The clandestine atmosphere of these escapades – the dark, the dew-damp grass under naked feet, the guilty taste of food on a green-stained tongue – heightened the metropolitan magic which in my view surrounded Henderson, who was often my partner on them. Once, however, we nearly had a quarrel. Something which he said had betrayed the fact that Henderson, in common with many of his contemporaries at that time (the mid-1930s), believed that babies were born out of their mothers' navels. I had already been given a rather sketchy version of 'the facts of life' and tried to convince him of his error, but with no success.

'Well, how *are* they born, then?' asked Henderson.

As I stumbled through an explanation, while we both stood shivering in the garden, his expression registered first bewilderment, then obstinacy, then scorn.

'You must be quite mad,' he said. 'I shouldn't tell anybody else what you've just told me if I were you or they might lock you away in a straitjacket and a padded cell and a jolly good job if they did too if you ask me.'

'I'm sure it's true,' I insisted, but with waning conviction.

'And I know that it isn't, so snubs. That's what navels are *for*, you *idiot*. Anyway, men and women aren't made in a different way like that.'

'But you can *see* that they are! Women have *paps*, don't they?'

'Oh, oh, thank you very much indeed, now we know, don't we?' said Henderson, jumping up and down in the moonlight and wagging his head wildly, as if drunk on his own sarcasm. 'Of *course* women have paps, but what's *that* got to do with anything, you *idiot*? They've got *cocks* too, just like we have.'

'Well, they *haven't*, that's all, I'm very sorry, and if you think they have that just shows how much *you* know about it.'

'I know they have,' said Henderson more seriously. 'I'm absolutely positive.' He turned away, and seemed ready to end the conversation.

'You don't know,' I taunted him, 'so don't tell lies.'

'I do know.'

'How?'

'Well, my mother's got one.'

'I bet she hasn't. Bet you anything.'

'Yes she has. I've seen it.'

'I don't believe you,' I said, beginning to feel uncomfortable.

'I slept in her room once when Daddy – when my father was away, to keep her company. She came in from the bath with nothing on and walked over to the dressing-table. I think she thought I was asleep but I wasn't. I was looking at her.'

That silenced me. Was Mrs Henderson some kind of a freak, then? Or could it be that her son was so reluctant to lose an argument that he had invented this extraordinary story about her? Or was it perhaps I who had been misinformed about the basic distinction between the sexes? In those days, at that age, it seemed that nothing to do with the subject was allowed to remain clear for long.

This was in fact one of very few occasions on which Henderson and I talked about sex, but our association was none the less disapproved of by Mr Philpots, the dormitory master, who presumably suspected that we discussed it all the time. He thought we had a bad influence on each other, giggled too much, were in some unspecified way 'silly', and if he caught us together he would try to break us up, indignantly muttering something about a 'mothers' meeting'. He was an unattractive old man and his nickname, Old Pisspots, suited him only too well. His baggy tweed plus-fours stank of stale tobacco, sweat and excrement; even his white hair and moustache had yellow stains as if splashed by his own urine. While one of his shaking hands was visibly engaged in a game of 'pocket billiards', the other would jerk out unexpectedly to tweak the nape of a pupil's neck. Too decrepit to teach, he spent most of his time in his own small room on the dormitory floor, into which he would sometimes invite one of the younger boys for a chat. He had his favourites, and Henderson was prime among these. Often, just before lights out, Henderson would be summoned in his pyjamas to the master's stuffy little cell, then after about ten minutes return in the dark and slip smoothly back into bed. Later, when most of the boys were asleep, Mr Philpots would come shambling along the passage in slippers and a greasy flannel dressing-gown to visit each dormitory in turn. He would make for the bed where his current favourite lay, and for minutes on end would address the sleeping figure in a scarcely audible monotone, mumbling terms of endearment and vague reproaches before gliding on like a grey somnambulist through the silent school.

If Henderson was Old Pisspot's pet, I was his *bête noire*. He was able to make life hard for me in many ways, but there was nothing he could do to prevent me from being 'taken out' by Henderson's parents one Sunday tea-time when they visited the school. Henderson himself had made it clear, while suggesting this excursion, that it had been their idea rather than his that he should invite a friend; they were apparently beginning to worry that he might not have any at all, and his desire to reassure them on this point must have outweighed his considerable embarrassment at the prospect of our social confrontation.

We were both ready, in stiff grey shorts and smelling of Honey and Flowers, when the Ford V8 drove up to the front door. Mr Henderson was at the wheel: with rabbit teeth beneath a toothbrush moustache, he resembled a *Punch* cartoon of a henpecked husband. Henderson briskly entered the front seat beside him, while I clambered into the back, where Mrs Henderson was sitting with an expensive-looking rug over her lap. She absently adjusted it to cover my knees as well, and the Ford moved off. I prayed that I wouldn't be car-sick or want to go to the lavatory.

Mrs Henderson came as a shock: she was a beauty. With the same pale complexion and blue-black hair as her son, she had a large drooping mouth and long violet eyes. Everything about her seemed to flop: her wide-brimmed hat, her scarf, her blouse, her long skirt and her long wrists. She appeared to be lost in a satisfied sulk and during the drive, as far as I can remember, nothing was said.

On a prickly common near a golf course, a sedate-looking establishment called The Three Monkeys sold garden teas. Mrs Henderson spread her car rug on the lawn and, after putting on a huge pair of purple-tinted sunglasses with white frames, lay down as if to sleep. Henderson and his father went off to play clock golf on the other side of the building, leaving me alone with Henderson's mother. It must often have happened, on similar outings, that a well-meaning adult has desperately tried to break through the reserve of a buttoned-up child. In our case, the roles were reversed. Mrs Henderson seemed either paralysed by shyness or overcome by apathy, while I for some reason could not stop talking. The only form of converse which I understood was that of question and answer: it was the first time I had consciously attempted to put another person at ease.

'What a nice scent you've got on,' I said.

'Thanks.'

'What's it called?'

'*Arpège*.'

'What's your favourite tune?'

For some seconds she gave this an almost solemn consideration. 'I think at the moment my *very* most favourite is a thing called "Would You?"'

'Who's your favourite film star?'

Again, she seemed to gather together all her powers of concentration to achieve a completely truthful answer. 'Either Robert Montgomery or Richard Arlen, I can't for certain say which.'

'That's a nice blouse you're wearing.'

'Thanks.'

'What's it made of?'

'*Crêpe de chine*.'

What I liked about Mrs Henderson was that, although she seemed so terribly bored, she didn't seem especially bored by me. She just didn't bother to take any extra trouble about me – an attitude which can be subtly flattering to an impatient child.

The tea-party was soon over: we had to be back at school by half past five. It seemed to me to have been a comparative success, but for some weeks afterwards Henderson avoided me. He probably guessed that his mother was much in my thoughts, and found the idea disturbing. Then, one morning, he came and stood beside me in the lavatory. 'I've had enough of this place,' he said after a while. 'I'm running away.'

'When?'

'Tonight. It's quite easy. I've worked it all out. Why don't you come too?'

At that moment the urinal flushed of its own

accord, making a hysterical hissing sound as if the mechanism were not completely under control. 'How will you get out?' I asked.

'The same way that we go to pick peas. Once we're gone there's nothing they can do to us. You can come home with me and ring up your people from there.'

'But how will you get to London?'

'Simple. If I don't get a lift all the way in a car there's an early train from Oxford station. Our flat isn't far from Paddington. I'll be home in time for breakfast. Eggs and bacon and Golden Shred.'

I let him give me detailed instructions about how and when and where we should meet.

That evening, after returning from his visit to Mr Philpots's room, Henderson did not get into bed but quietly put on his day clothes instead. Then he left the dormitory without a glance in my direction. I covered my head with the sheet and stared at the luminous dial of my Mickey Mouse wristwatch. After five minutes I followed Henderson downstairs to the changing-room. He was waiting patiently by the window. When he saw me, he frowned. 'But you're not dressed,' he said.

'I'm not coming with you.'

'You're too frightened,' he stated. I did not deny the accusation, although I felt incoherently that the truth was somehow more complicated than this.

'Oh, well, never mind, I'm going just the same.' His features had settled in a stubborn look which I remembered from earlier arguments, and I did not attempt to make him change his mind.

Henderson raised the lower sash and eased his

body through the aperture. I stood at the window and watched him make his escape, scampering across the moonlit playing fields, over a low stone wall and on to the open road. When he had disappeared from view I went cautiously back to bed. Mixed emotions – remorse, relief, intense excitement – prevented me from sleeping and I was still awake hours later when Old Pisspots came shuffling down the passage. He stood for a while at the entrance to the room, his head trembling as he greedily swallowed his excess spittle, before moving as usual towards Henderson's empty bed. In the dim light its rumpled condition made it appear occupied to the besotted schoolmaster's rheumy eyes. He began to whisper. This time I could make out most of the words.

'Darling boy, darling imp, darling scamp, *what* a bad lad! Oh, you little rogue, what do you mean by sleeping like that, my darling, as if butter wouldn't melt in your mouth, you naughty, naughty boy? Oh, I'll wager somebody had a sore bottom, somebody had a tender behind, didn't he, darling? Couldn't sit down for a week, eh? Not after having your little sit-upon spanked for you, what? What? Never mind, little boy, there's nothing the matter with a good old-fashioned ... and you did ask for it, you know, didn't you, darling? Such a cheeky little arab. What a sauce, eh? Well, if you still have an aching bum in the morning, don't you come running to me, darling, wanting to kiss and make up, what? Oh, my darling ...'

The dormitory windows whitened and he muttered on. I heard the desolate whistle and purposeful rumble of the milk train as it crossed a distant viaduct. Could Henderson conceivably be on it? It suddenly struck me that he had no money to buy a ticket. More likely, he had hitched a ride on some lorry and was now journeying along the Great West Road, past deserted factories and pallid petrol stations, towards his native London with its cavernous cinemas and subterranean nightclubs. Was he in panic-stricken flight or on an adventurous voyage of discovery? I only knew that Henderson was going back home to his mother, that aloof hermaphrodite and elegant sphinx, who carried beneath scented *crêpe de chine* pyjamas the threat of her phallic secret.

Obsessions

'C'est ce que j'ai d'inhabile, d'incertain, qui est bien moi-même.'

Paul Valéry, *Extraits du Log-Book de Monsieur Teste*

I still dream about the Manor, although I have not seen it for over thirty years and could not have entered it more than a dozen times in the days when I lived near by. In fact I have almost forgotten what it looked like, but can just recall the disturbing impression made on me by some hidden harmony in the relationship of its passages, staircases and rooms; and this subliminal memory sometimes surfaces through my sleep to form an incongruous though unsurprising background to people and problems that belong to later stages in my life.

More haunting than haunted, it was a placidly beautiful house, built in the reign of Charles II and set in a small park; on one side the grounds sloped to a valley where a trout stream ran through soggy watermeadows and on the other a softly wooded hill rose to the gusty downs. People who cared about furniture made pilgrimages in the hope of seeing inside it, but these were obdurately discouraged by the owner, Sir Jocelyn Bignall, who attached no aesthetic value to his inherited possessions although he would never have allowed the slightest displacement in their arrangement: the interior of the Manor had therefore remained more or less unaltered since the seventeenth century, preserved by the lazy philistinism and disinclination for change which characterised Sir Jocelyn and his ancestors. Over seventy when I knew him, he was like a clumsy caricature of the old-fashioned country squire, with pendulous purple cheeks matching the loud purple checks on his expensively tailored knickerbocker suits. He had the reputation in the village of being a very bad landlord, and had until lately been Master of the local Fox Hounds.

Sir Jocelyn was seldom seen at home because he got on his wife's nerves; she invariably addressed him in a hectoring, querulous tone and would sometimes openly dismiss him from the room if he happened to be found there when friends came to see her. A small, pretty old lady with bad-tempered features almost obliterated by powder, Lady Bignall modelled her appearance on the 'Marquise' look exemplified by Dame Marie Tempest and always wore a wig which, like a barrister's, was clearly not intended to deceive. An ancient Edwardian scandal, not yet quite forgotten in some pockets of the neighbourhood, surrounded the origins of their association with improbable romance. Lady Bignall (whose first name, by fateful coincidence, was also Jocelyn) had abandoned a former husband and 'bolted' with Sir Jocelyn to Boulogne. There had either been an unpleasantly protracted divorce, or else no divorce at all until the first husband died; in any event, the lovers had been forced to live openly together for some years at the Manor before becoming man and wife. It was rumoured that, had it not been for this equivocal episode in his past, Sir Jocelyn would have long ago been Lord-Lieutenant of the county.

The Bignalls were childless, but Lady Bignall had a daughter by her first marriage who often stayed at the Manor. Madge had married a soldier much older than herself; General Sir Archie Fuller was indeed nearly the same age as Sir Jocelyn. The Fullers had one son, named after his grandmother and therefore confusingly called Jocelyn too. Lady Bignall doted on him, but when he came to the Manor he spent most of his time fishing or shooting with old Sir Jocelyn while she sat impatiently indoors with her daughter.

Madge Fuller had a tall, slim body ideally suited to the clothes in fashion during the early 1930s, which she continued to wear long after they had gone out of date. Fur-trimmed collars seemed to raise her shoulders while her trunk was apparently lowered by skirts reaching below the calf, so that she gave an effect of elegant but painful attenuation, as if she had been stretched on a rack. On each occasion that I saw her she was wearing the same hat – or, at least, an identical copy of the original: a simple beret, part of which had been folded over on itself and fastened to the side of her head by a jewelled regimental brooch. Her manner was one of eager, almost avid welcome combined with exaggerated deprecation. Something aggrieved inside her drove her to disparage and apologise for every aspect of her own personality: she refused to allow that anything belonging to herself could be deserving of praise. This category included both her husband and, to a lesser extent, her son.

It may have been because he was now hers that she hated Sir Archie so fiercely; or perhaps she had disliked him on sight and her marriage (no doubt 'arranged' by the worldly and slightly *déclassée* Lady Bignall) had left her with a sense of disappointment which had developed into generalised resentment and eventually narrowed to a violent self-distrust. She treated him with even greater contempt than her mother showed for Sir Jocelyn, and persistently complained about his crass stupidity – even to people, like myself, who had never been given the chance to meet him. This behaviour was, I believe, much criticised by her acquaintances, but Lady Fuller's loathing for Sir Archie was too strong to be denied expression by conventional opinion.

I went to the same public school as Jocelyn Fuller, but since he was four years older than I was we seldom came into contact and I only knew him there from a distance as an imposingly mature figure who excelled at games. One day I saw him trotting down a path towards me: I stood aside to let him pass, but he stopped and spoke. 'My mother's descending on the school next Sunday, and she'd love to see you. We're having tea at the Cockpit. Can you join us?'

In great confusion, I heard myself accepting the

invitation, and as he turned away I immediately began to dread this engagement which I knew would be beyond my power to fulfil. As it happened, I had already obtained permission to go to London that Sunday for the afternoon, on the pretext of visiting a relation; but the real reason for my panic was more irrational. I was suffering from that mysterious self-consciousness which often attacks the adolescent, a malady as agonising and overwhelming as seasickness or stage fright.

My dilemma was acute: I could no more show up at the Cockpit than I could see a way of getting out of the obligation. Moral paralysis drove me to the extreme course of seeking my housemaster's advice. He was probably amused when my problem turned out to be social rather than sexual or spiritual, but he gave it serious attention. 'It's nothing to worry about. If you feel too shy to tell Fuller that you made a mistake, why don't you drop him a note? Just explain that you've already arranged to spend Sunday with your people.'

'But what shall I *call* him in the note?'

'What do you call him in the holidays?'

'Jocelyn, I suppose, if anything–but I really hardly know him at all.'

'I think it would be all right to call him Jocelyn in your letter.'

In the end I disregarded this suggestion and began the note with the formal address 'Dear Fuller'. After I had furtively left it at Jocelyn's house, choosing a time when I knew he would be on the playing fields, I felt delirious with relief. On Sunday I took a train to Paddington and went by myself to see Alice Faye in *Alexander's Ragtime*

Band. A tune from the film took root in my brain where it lingered sweetly as a constant accompaniment and frequent alternative to thought. *Now it can be told ... Told in all its glory ... Now that we have met the world may know the ... Sentimental story ...*

Not long after this, when during the holidays I was asked to lunch at the Manor to meet Lady Fuller and Jocelyn, I felt no qualms about accepting: my hysteria had belonged to the unnatural and inhibiting atmosphere of boarding-school life. I walked the half mile from the village to the stone gates surmounted by subtly grotesque lions' heads, their prophetic grandeur if anything increased by their weather-beaten and dilapidated condition, up the long drive past unmown grass to the crystalline façade, unnerving in its symmetry. Lady Fuller came anxiously to meet me at the front door and led me to the Chinoiserie room where her mother was perkily waiting. Sir Jocelyn was away somewhere, fulfilling his duties as a magistrate.

'It's such a treat for *my* Jocelyn', said Lady Fuller, 'to meet somebody of his own age for a change. You will be kind to him, won't you? He's not very intellectual, you know, and I'm afraid you may be too fearfully bored. But we'll try and make it up to you by giving you an edible meal!'

Jocelyn joined us, wearing white flannels; his friendly, candid face looked rather sweaty. 'Very sporty-boy!' said Lady Bignall with approval. 'Come on, let's all have a little drinksky-korsakoff.' Jocelyn poured us each a glass of sherry before we moved into the dining-room.

During lunch, Lady Fuller started a discussion on the dullness of country life. 'One's neighbours are apt to be so frightfully stuffy, unless one's unusually lucky. Sometimes I do rather hanker after London. A little house in Chelsea would be my dream – but then you see I adore being near water.'

'Mummy's a highbrow at heart,' said Jocelyn flirtatiously.

'I've no idea what Chelsea's like now,' said Lady Bignall, 'but in my day it used to be full of bounderinos.'

'One feels in such a backwater, stuck out in the wilds,' Lady Fuller continued. 'How one longs to know what's going on in the rest of the world! Oh, one reads the papers and listens to the six o'clock news, but it isn't quite the same. I do find things so terribly difficult to understand at the moment, don't you? The world situation is getting so complicated and I'm dying for somebody to *explain* it to me. Needless to say, when it comes to that sort of thing, Archie's no more good than a sick headache!'

'It would be fun to dash across to Monte or Juan for a spell and get a change of ideas,' said Lady Bignall. 'But *he* won't budge, so what's the use? And they tell me I wouldn't recognise the Riviera now – full of cads and Americans, I suppose, just like everywhere else.'

At the end of the meal, while her mother was pouring out coffee, Madge Fuller turned to me with an urgent expression on her face. 'I *do* hope you haven't succumbed to this ghastly custom I find now all over the place of going *back* into the drawing-room after luncheon and drinking your coffee there! I really cannot stand it: it seems to me to be such a mad idea! It quite takes away the whole point of having coffee at all if one has to move all the way from one room to another before one can get at it. I can't understand why everybody doesn't see what I mean about this – but apparently they don't. The most surprising people seem to be catching the habit. It's just the sort of thing that drives me absolutely *crackers*!' she finished wildly, then paused, panting slightly, before adding on a brisker note: 'Now, why don't you two boys go off together somewhere for a good talk? Jocelyn is starved for conversation with people of his own generation, aren't you, darling? But you mustn't bore our guest, whatever you do: I sometimes think that being a bore is *the* unforgivable sin, do you know what I mean? Anything but that!'

I followed Jocelyn upstairs and into his bedroom. He wandered about for a bit with an abstracted air, as if he were alone, and then stood for a time at a window, looking out at the park. Embarrassed, I lowered myself into a chair. 'That's right,' he said, 'sit down, sit down, for goodness' sake.' He turned and gazed at me with blank gravity and then unexpectedly flung himself on to the bed and stared with the same absent concentration at the ceiling. I could think of nothing to say: the silence was not unpleasant, but I perversely longed to break it.

Suddenly Jocelyn rolled round on the bed and lifted himself into a squatting position, supported by his knees and elbows with his face against the pillow and his bottom companionably in the air. 'Would you say that Flora Robson was a great actress?' he asked. 'She is very good,' I replied. He went on, his voice rather muffled: 'I saw her in that thing where she was meant to be Queen Elizabeth. Extraordinary woman, Queen Elizabeth, quite remarkable, a great queen, wouldn't you say? So was Queen Victoria in her way, I suppose, but I've always thought they must have been rather a stuffy pair, Prince Albert and her, do you know what I mean? She was a great queen but she must have been awfully stuffy and Victorian.'

'Do you think Flora Robson would be good as Queen Victoria?' I said at random. He raised his head from the pillow and turned it round to peer in my direction. 'I *wonder*,' he mused. 'I *wonder*. That's quite a thought. Quite a thought.' Then he leaped off the bed and ran his fingers through his hair, mildly massaging his scalp. 'Let's go down and see if Gan-Gan can rustle us up some tea. We *have* had a lovely talk. It's very nice staying here and all that but I do miss the company of people my own age. Elderly folk can be awfully stuffy, can't they? You must come over again soon.'

Later that year the war started, and I heard that Jocelyn had gone straight from school into the army. Lady Bignall boasted of his rapid promotion and military success: he was in something very dangerous and dashing, but so 'hush-hush' that it could only be described in the vaguest terms. She would sit in the Chinoiserie room beside the wireless and listen to the news. This was often bad, but Lady Bignall refused to be depressed. 'It all depends on the value you put on human life,' she said. 'I've been reading a lot of eastern philosophy lately and I've learnt that it's a great mistake to put too much value on human life. Anyway, you don't want to believe everything you hear on the wireless ... Madge writes that she thanks heaven Archie's too old for a command: with him a Brass Hat we'd be *certain* to lose the war!'

As it turned out, I was one of the last people to see Sir Jocelyn alive. I spent a long, tedious afternoon acting as an amateurish beater on a shoot consisting of only two guns – Sir Jocelyn and his friend and contemporary, Admiral Bovill. (The Admiral and Lady Bignall did not get on: he thought her 'flighty' and she considered him 'much too churchy'.) We trudged over the countryside while the old men slap-happily blazed away, missing every bird, and I diverted myself by singing 'Now It Can Be Told', still my favourite song, in a tuneless undertone. We reached a river where, on the opposite bank, the dead body of an otter was pathetically exposed. The Admiral crept stealthily up to the water's edge and, after taking careful aim, fired in its direction. When we returned at dusk to the Manor, the otter's putrefying corpse (which I had to carry) was the only trophy of our chase. 'Glad you got that otter, Admiral,' said Sir Jocelyn. 'Adds a bit of variety to the bag!' That night, he died in his sleep. I laboured for days over my letter of condolence to his widow, which in the end proved too difficult to write and was never posted.

I left school as soon as I decently could and filled in time before the inevitable call-up by going to

Oxford. The minimum academic qualification was needed for this: the university was only half full. My rooms there were large and gloomy, furnished darkly in carved oak with monumental dressers, creaking wardrobes and sinister sideboards. I was too depressed by the present, too fearful of the future, to do any work at all. At night a mouse would emerge from the shadows and play by my feet in the chilly grate. One evening, without my knowledge, a college servant set a trap for it; in the morning the cheese was gone with the trap still unsprung, and that night the mouse confidently returned. My days were spent in the cinema or changing library books at Elliston & Cavell's, where a branch of the Times Book Club, to which I subscribed, was then accommodated. I had developed a mania for the work of Mignon G. Eberhart, an American author of detective stories, and could read nothing else. Her books, like the films of Alice Faye, were so similar to each other that they might have seemed almost indistinguishable to an untrained eye, but subtle differences between them added piquancy to the expert's taste. Some of her earlier novels were difficult to find, and I would advertise for these in the trade papers. Just as the dreaded moment arrived when I had read them all, a new one was published by the Crime Club. I bought it at W. H. Smith's and, deciding that my future presence in Oxford was unnecessary, went back home about halfway through my first term.

There I found a letter awaiting me. It was from Madge Fuller, who explained that she had sent it to this address in the hope that it might be forwarded, as she was uncertain about which college I attended. She would be passing through Oxford in a few days' time, staying at the Mitre: would I care to dine with her there on Sunday evening? She ended in her old aggressively humble vein by writing that if I was much too busy swotting for Little Go, or just too bored by the prospect of spending an evening in her company, she would of course quite understand and I mustn't dream of coming. 'For goodness' sake don't bother to answer – a telephone message with the hall porter will do. I'll expect you if I see you!'

Once again, her well-intended offer of hospitality had placed me in a dilemma. The local myth of my status as an industrious student must at all costs be maintained before Lady Bignall, a fertile source of much disapproving gossip. At home I felt in hiding, on the run from some self-imposed standard of normal behaviour; my refuge was dangerously near to Lady Bignall, but this of course had been an unavoidable risk. Now Lady Fuller, impelled by her chronically tactless generosity, had innocently stumbled on my secret and flushed me out of my retreat. So I embarked on another of those desolate wartime Sunday travels: the bus from the village to the market town; the slow, crowded train to Didcot; the long, hungry wait at the junction; the brutally prolonged discomfort of the last lap. 'Well may they ask', I thought, 'if this journey is really necessary.' I walked downhill from Oxford station as light-headed and disorientated as a dreamer or a drunk.

Lady Fuller was waiting for me just inside the entrance to the Mitre. She immediately began apologising for her presumption in taking me away from my studies. 'You must be so fearfully busy: I know how hard they make one work here. Now whatever happens, you mustn't let me *bore* you – when one's always surrounded by stupid people, one becomes such an idiot oneself! The least I can do in return is to offer you a decent meal, but I expect it will be *uneatable*, don't you?' She hurried me into the dining-room, where she sat for some time gazing at the menu with the air of someone meeting a challenge, as if it were at the same time intensely interesting and almost impossible to comprehend. She seemed to be in a state of nervous exaltation, and I thought that this could possibly be accounted for by the mere fact of her presence in Oxford, which she no doubt saw as the palpable embodiment of her cerebral ideal. Here she was, sitting in a seat of learning: I suddenly remembered that I was an undergraduate, and for the first time understood that this designation could carry symbolic overtones as potent as those of soldier, prostitute or priest.

After ordering the set dinner, she loosened her silver-fox, snapped open the clips of her crocodile handbag and cosily rummaged inside it for a gold cigarette case and lighter; then she began to pack the former with the contents of a bright red packet of Craven A. The regimental brooch sparkled on her bent-over beret: beneath it, her eyes fixed me with a kindly fanaticism. 'Now, you've got to tell me what the *young* are thinking about things, what they're reading, what they admire. You've no idea how I envy you being in touch with ideas. It must be so wonderfully exciting – I don't know when I last met anybody who had an idea in his *head*! How I wish I were brainy, like you (yes, you are, you know you are, you must be), because I do think, more and more, that in the end it's only brains that count. So do tell me, who are the really clever young men of your generation? I'm sure you must know them all.'

I tried to change the subject by asking after Jocelyn, who was now said to be the youngest major in the British Army and had recently been decorated, but she refused to be side-tracked and insisted on an answer. What did I tell her? I can't remember. Whatever it was must have struck her as bitterly inadequate, but she was too polite to show her disappointment. Perhaps my feeble, evasive replies only confirmed her modest belief that the intellectual life would always remain impenetrable to the uninitiated, a teasing riddle with a simple solution which lay just beyond the confines of her understanding. Anyhow, she seemed fairly satisfied. When the meal was eaten she leant towards me and said, with a jocular air of conspiracy: '*Shall we risk the coffee?*'

'I'd love some.'

'You're sure you have time? You're not dying to get back to your work? It will probably be simply filthy but we can always hope for the best.'

It was some time before the waiter responded to her signals; and then he told her the last thing she wanted to hear. 'Coffee is served in the lounge, madam.'

She caught my eye with a grimace signifying an only partly humorous despair. 'Rubbish! Surely I'm entitled to drink my cup of after-dinner coffee where I choose to? I'm staying at your hotel, you know, and this young man is my guest.' The elderly waiter repeated that he had to obey the rule, which was apparently quite inflexible.

Madge Fuller bullied him for a bit and then changed her tactic to one of seductive charm. She seemed to be trying to lure him into partnership with her on some voluptuously dangerous design as she pleaded with him, just this once, to break the establishment's repressive and unnecessary law. When this method failed too, she started to lose her self-control: indignation gave way to a rather frightening distress. She demanded an interview with the manager, and after a long delay was told that the manager could not be found. Beside herself with irritation, she repeated her protest like a litany: 'I will *not* drink coffee in the lounge! It's *so* much nicer at the table! It *ruins* the meal to have to move!' Alarmed and exhausted, the waiter began at last to back gingerly away from her, and then vanished altogether through the service door. She sat there implacably, as though on an unofficial strike for some doomed but high-principled cause.

'You do think I'm right, don't you? I mean, it only encourages them if one gives in. In *no other country* would one be prevented from drinking one's coffee at the dining table. It's typical of England, I'm afraid: no wonder it looks as if we're going to lose this ridiculous war! I do most *abjectly* apologise – it's too awful, you haven't had any coffee! But even if we *did* go into the lounge (which God forbid – what a ghastly word anyhow, *lounge*!) we'd be stuck there for hours because the service in hotels nowadays is practically non-existent, and I couldn't bear the guilt of feeling that I was keeping you away from your books. You've probably got exams coming up soon: now promise me you won't sit up all night preparing for them. I'm sure you've been working much too hard. You do look a little peaky – you'll only get brain-fag if you overdo it, you know.'

It could not have been more than eight o'clock when I left the Mitre – disconcertingly early, for my day was done. The town seemed empty and echoing, like a concrete swimming pool drained of water. I walked haltingly back to my rooms, postponing my return because I knew no novel by Mignon G. Eberhart (not even one already familiar) awaited me there. All bookshops and libraries were closed: I felt the throbbing onset of the addict's withdrawal pains. How would I get through the night? I made myself a cup of Nescafé and went wide awake to bed.

It was some years later, when the war was won and life had changed for the better, that I began to dream about the Manor.

The Half Brother

Jack 'did a Jack' and missed our father's funeral. He had taken his new girl to the Gargoyle Club the night before and had woken with such a monumental hangover that the train had left Paddington before he was out of bed. Explaining this to my mother on the telephone later in the day, he had boasted not only about the hangover but also about the new girl, who was just seventeen and had a marvellous figure – almost like a boy's. The joke was that he had been given twenty-four hours' compassionate leave *because* of the funeral. 'Father would have been amused,' he said.

'Oh darling, I'm almost glad you weren't there,' said my mother. 'It was a nightmare: you couldn't have borne it. Lady Bignall kept on saying: "What are your plans?" Wasn't that typical?'

'Typical,' said Jack. 'How Father would have laughed.'

'I can't stand it when people ask me about my plans ... Oh, Jack, isn't it *awful*, feeling awful?'

'Awful,' said her stepson. On this subject he was indeed an acknowledged expert, and there existed a list of proscribed places (Villefranche, Sao Tome, Bordighera, Colwyn Bay) where Jack had experienced – with an intensity that elevated them into family legend – the dusty depths of *le cafard*.

In order to take Jack's call, my mother had been forced to re-enter my father's study because that was where the telephone was. During the last weeks of his illness my father's bed had been moved downstairs to this seldom-used room: it was here that my mother had nursed him and here that he had died. The appearance of the bed in the study had been disturbing from the start, as confusedly ominous as a phrase out of context; now, stripped and desolate, it just looked pointless. One of its sides was set against a low bookcase which ran the length of the wall. This contained, among other 'uniform editions', the complete works of Turgenev, in fourteen tall grey volumes, translated by Isabel F. Hapgood. (My father had been military attaché at St Petersburg before the revolution, and *A Sportsman's Sketches* was his favourite book.) The top of the bookcase formed a bedside shelf, on which bottles of chalky medicine and boxes of little green pills were still scattered among the few art objects surviving from Stars, the vast Victorian Gothic pile near Salisbury Plain where my father had been born. These included Chinese porcelain bowls of *pot-pourri*, enamel icons by Alexander Fisher and a life-sized effigy of Horus, the ancient Egyptian god of the sky in the shape of a falcon, whose right eye was the Sun and whose left eye was the Moon. Fashioned out of dark rough stone, this squat and sinister statuette concealed beneath its flat tail a tiny trapdoor which opened on to a dusty cavity housing the brittle yellow bones, supposedly undisturbed since the second century BC, of the original bird.

Talking to Jack had upset my mother. The telephone was navy blue, shaped like a daffodil with a flimsy bracket protruding sideways from its upright stem: she had difficulty in replacing the receiver on this when their conversation was over. She was crying. 'Darling Jack,' she said. 'His voice sounded so like Yvo's. He's coming down as soon as he can ...' She looked distractedly round the room and her gaze was arrested by sight of the falcon. 'Do you know, I'm sure that bird brings bad luck. I've always thought it was creepy but Yvo did love it so ... It was next to his bed when he died: now I *know* it's unlucky. Oh, please, do help me to get rid of it!'

'You mean, throw it away?'

'Or sell it, or something. I know that Yvo always laughed at me for being superstitious, but I am sure that Jack would understand.'

Jack and I were half-brothers, although he was old enough to be my father. Jack's mother had died of influenza in 1919 and four years later the widower had surprised and relieved his son by a second marriage, this time to somebody much younger than himself: indeed, my mother was an exact contemporary of Jack's. My father retired from the War Office to a small house in Berkshire where my mother started a chicken farm and I was born. Jack had recently inherited Stars, left to him by a cousin in a will which overlooked my father in order to avoid unnecessary death duties; when the will was made it had seemed unlikely that my father would remarry and even more so that the cousin would die so young. Jack offered to give Stars to my father, who refused it: in return, Jack undertook to pay for my education. As things turned out, this promise was not kept.

Jack soon sold Stars (which became first a secretarial college and then a lunatic asylum before mysteriously burning down) and most of its contents; for a brief period he was a very rich young man. He had had a sad time at boarding school while my father was soldiering abroad, and a grim time as a subaltern during the First World War; now he was doggedly determined to have a *good* time at last. His money was spent on racing cars, aeroplanes, a famous wine cellar, a collection of 'modern' pictures and a series of difficult, exquisite girls. He enjoyed among his contemporaries a comfortable reputation for privileged Bohemianism, scandalising some by his licentious behaviour and distressing others by his 'arty' inclinations, but avoiding the kind of unpopularity that might threaten his status as a proud member of White's Club. When my father died, the Second World War was ending and Jack, nearly fifty, was broke.

On the day after the funeral, my mother returned to the subject of the falcon. By now she had succeeded in infecting me with her sense of urgency in the matter, which just stopped short of panic. So this is what I did. I packed Horus in a cardboard egg-box (before petrol rationing she used to sell eggs to Quaglino's, nipping up to London and back in the Baby Austin while my father anxiously awaited her return) and caught the carrier to Hungerford station. After an hour the uptrain sidled in: Kintbury, Newbury,

Thatcham, Aldermaston, Theale, Reading West ... from Reading it was non-stop to London. My arms aching, I queued for another hour before a taxi took me to a shop in St James's called Spink's. There I asked to see an expert on Egyptian art. He was quite young, with white lashes. I unpacked the antique. He offered me a hundred pounds for it, which I happily accepted. Free of my sacred burden, I wandered round the capital: saw an old film called *Naples au Baiser du Feu* at Studio One, then gravitated down Oxford Street to Bumpus where I stole a novel by I. Compton-Burnett (I think it must have been *Elders and Betters*) before catching the six o'clock home. The whole transaction was accomplished during a halting adolescent reverie, and I never gave a thought to Jack. There, I was to discover, I had made a mistake.

He turned up one morning about a fortnight later, having commandeered an army jeep at Devizes, where he had been attending a course exclusively for majors. Throughout the 1930s, Jack's arrivals at our village had been god-like: emerging, goggled, from a long low Bentley with hyperthyroid headlights; or descending on to the local football pitch at the bottom of Spring's Hill in a skeletal flying machine, only too aptly named a Moth and disconcertingly reminiscent of the expensive toys from Hamleys with which he embarrassed my birthdays. This latest visitation, though inevitably less glamorous, was in a subtle way just as dramatic. Jack's tall gaunt trunk and unevenly articulated limbs managed to banish from his battledress any suggestion of a uniform; his peaked cap concealed his bald crown and dignified the wild, woolly white hair round his neck and ears. He climbed out of the jeep, stretched, belched, pissed against a cedar in the drive and proposed a walk to his favourite pub in a hamlet ten miles away.

Jack was a pub snob. He wouldn't be seen dead in a saloon bar, and many were the authentic 'publics' I'd sat in with him, surrounded by fascist farm-hands and their goitred mothers-in-law, dodging the dangerous darts as they sped from dainty thumb and forefinger to the pitted corky board, trying to master the rules of cribbage ('One for his nob') and staggering, beer-bloated, to the Gents – a midge-haunted half-wall of cement in a benighted backyard.

'But you've only just got here!' said my mother. 'There's plenty of drink in the house . . . I've talked to the Manor and you can fish there whenever you want.'

'Wonderful!' said Jack. 'I'll walk up as soon as we've had our lunch. All right, then, let's forget about the pub. I can stay till tomorrow morning: any exciting plans for tonight?'

'There's a film on in Hungerford with Hedy Lamarr,' I suggested.

'Or we might have some bridge, if I can get hold of the Admiral,' said my mother.

'Bridge!' Jack decided. 'Hedy Lamarr must be as old as Methuselah by now.'

He entered the house, accompanied as ever (or so I felt) by an invisible spirit of pure hedonism which quickened the atmosphere with its promise of an extended treat while setting an unnervingly high standard for any prospective participant.

There seemed to exist a law (as far as one knew, unwritten) forbidding the world to subject Jack to one moment of boredom; to be in his company was to share in the privilege thus afforded, while running the risk of breaking the law oneself. He poured himself a large whisky and soda and, after some galvanic contortions, settled himself beside it on a sofa; my mother and I prepared ourselves contentedly for the fun his presence always guaranteed.

Jack's dissipated past revealed itself in his face and made him look almost twenty years older than his age, but in spite of this there was still something boyish about him, both in behaviour and appearance. His candid enthusiasm, his ungovernable touchiness, retained an adolescent innocence; the clumsy movements of his bony body suggested the physical uncertainty of a child rather than the stumblings of an elderly party. Behind the benevolent beam, or offended scowl, of a grizzled patriarch, the short nose, wide smile and cleft chin evoked the attractive lad, cheeky and vulnerable by turns, that he must once have been.

He had loved, but been shy of, my father, and their relationship had never fully emerged from a crippling cocoon of embarrassed reserve. With my mother he could be more comfortably – even cosily – affectionate, treating her as he might have done a sister, with genuine respect, artless trust and a touch of amused condescension. Their cordial intercourse had given birth to several family jokes, the ritual repetition of which bound them yet closer together. Both belonged to – had indeed invented – the Four O'Clock in the Morning

Club, whose insomniac members were entitled to ring each other up at that lonely hour. These healing conversations might largely consist of warnings about an imminent New Moon, for they shared a fanatic belief in the danger of glimpsing such a phenomenon through intervening glass. (Spectacles, and on occasion windshields, they decided, 'didn't count'.) Their attitudes towards superstition were alike: serious to the point of solemnity, but moderated by an enjoyably guilty sense of the absurdity in abandoning rationality to this vertiginous extent. It was in fact the silliness of the traditional taboos (involving ladders, cats and salt) that attracted them, while in some complex fashion deepening their faith, as if they felt it fitting that so cruel and arbitrary a mystery as fate should provide clues to its intentions and means of forestalling them in banal or frivolous forms. A favourite family joke was about Jack saying one morning: 'Did you hear a terrible crash in the middle of the night? Well, that was me, touching wood!'

We were therefore astonished by the violence of Jack's reaction when my mother told him (in a thoughtless aside during her account of the recent horror of her husband's last illness and the present misery of her bereavement) about her sudden dread of Horus and impulsive decision to sell it. He started up in his seat, accidentally kicking over the tumbler which contained his whisky and soda: the glass shattered and the drink seeped into the threadbare Aubusson carpet, leaving a stain similar to those already made by the messes of Martha, my father's favourite dachshund. His face had gone stony with fury and his voice had acquired a barely intelligible parade-ground bark. 'No, it's not true! You can't have done! I don't believe it! Jesus Christ, this is just too bloody much! My dear girl, all I can say is, I only hope you never realise exactly what you've ... I mean, what in the name of? ... of all the imperial *idiots*! ... to do such a damn fool thing ... why on earth didn't you consult me first? Would that have been too much to expect? That statuette was the *only* object of any *real* value among all the rubbish which my grand-parents collected at Stars. What did you get for it? A measly hundred quid? Clearly you've been swindled ... God *knows* what it's worth, but that's not my point, my point is that it's a fantastically beautiful thing in itself, a work of *art*, for Christ's sake! But I suppose that means nothing to you – it can't do – well that's not your fault, I see that, but the thing that I *can't* get over is that you knew perfectly well that Father *adored* it. You had no *right* – neither of you did – to get rid of it like that without letting me know. Apart from anything else, I'd have treasured it as something to remember Father by – I haven't anything else of his. He was my father too, you know!'

My mother stared at Jack as if he had gone mad. Incapable of speech, she hurried unsteadily from the room and out of the front door. We could see her, through the window, wandering about the garden, as if distractedly seeking some means of escape. I wanted to join her but felt paralysed by shock. Jack's neck and cheeks were rust-red; he looked as if he were about to weep. When at last he spoke, his voice was husky but softer and the tone was no longer bullying but one of rough comradeship–man-to-man. 'Shit, I seemed to have spilt my fucking drink! Pour me another one, will you, there's a good chap. Sorry about that outburst—but women can be such *cunts* sometimes, can't they? You'd better explain exactly where you took the sodding thing.'

I did so, and then he strode outside to apologise to my mother: from the porch I watched them embrace. His visit was spoilt, but not irreparably ruined. He fished all afternoon and spent the evening listening to Mozart on the radiogram; he left before breakfast on the following day. A week later, he rang up from a call-box, reversing the charge. I answered the telephone. Jack told me that he had been up to London and bought back the falcon fron Spink's. 'But they really jewed me—charged me a hundred and ten for it. I make that a clear profit of ten per cent for them. But never mind, all's well that end's well! There go the pips . . . Goodbye!'

The private nursing home was near Sloan Square. I found Jack on the first floor in a large, high-ceilinged Edwardian room furnished only by a narrow bed, a small table with a Bible attached to it on a chain, an easy chair upholstered in a jazz pattern of oatmeal and chocolate, an immense wardrobe of carved oak, and a chromium-fitted wash basin of aggressively clinical appearance. Wearing a voluminous jibbah, he was standing with his back to me looking out of the window at a white building of oriental design across the road.

'Wouldn't you say that was some sort of mosque?' he said. 'Well, it isn't. Apparently it's a Christian Scientist church!' He gave a hearty, social laugh and gazed round the room in an uncertain way, as though it were he and not I who had just entered it for the first time.

He had been incarcerated here for ten days, 'drying out'. A popular doctor of the day specialised in curing alcoholics by a series of injections intended to stimulate those cells of the brain where in his opinion a congenital debility had caused the original craving, combined with a brutal form of aversion therapy. On starting the treatment, a patient named his poison – whisky, gin, brandy, rum, champagne: Jack had opted for whisky. From then on, this was the only liquid available to him; if the gleaming new wash basin had functioned at all, whisky would have spouted from its taps; while regular and supervised intakes of an emetic called antabuse guaranteed that every sip of it would make him vomit. The doctor had achieved some spectacular successes by this method, and it looked as if it had worked with Jack. He had telephoned earlier in the week, asking for some clean clothes, his chequebook and some ready cash to be brought round to Wilbraham Place as they were letting him leave that morning and he had a lunch date at the Étoile with a promising girl.

I put the suitcase on his bed. 'Here are the things you wanted.'

'Thank you, darling,' he said absentmindedly.

Over the past three years, since demobilisation from the Army, things had gone badly for Jack.

His formerly flamboyant style cramped by money worries, he had found it hard to cash in on any one of his several remarkable gifts; unlike the 1920s, this second post-war period had so far shown few signs of favouring the dilettante. One of his love affairs had taken a fatally serious turn: he had become obsessed by a young woman and continued to be so long after she had grown tired of him and left him for somebody else. This setback had bred in him neurotic fears about loss of potency; groundless at first, they had perversely sapped his confidence to a point where they seemed to be justified. It had not taken long, in this discouraging atmosphere, for the epicurean wine-lover, honoured by the Wine and Food Society for his wide knowledge and discriminating palate, to degenerate into a drunk; but the degeneration was only partial, and Jack was a drunk determined to be cured.

To fetch the suitcase and some of its contents, I had travelled down on the previous day to his lovely, melancholy mill house by a Sussex marsh, scene of many fabulous orgies, treasure hunts and fancy-dress balls between the wars. Set in a damp, wooded hollow, its picturesque little rooms, once hung with nudes by Modigliani and Matisse, were echo-less though empty. I turned the pages of the Visitors' Book, where liverish guests had attempted to write witty comments on the food, the drink and the company after those famous weekend parties that had sounded so enviable to the uninvited. Many of these inscriptions contained private or topical references and no longer made sense to an outsider, but 'Widows are wonderful!' clearly celebrated Jack's Veuve Cliquot, and one of his literary friends had composed an ingenious anacreontic about a prizewinning hang-over. As I walked away from the house, down the sloping croquet lawn to the silver pool, over the rickety bridge across the tranquil stream and up the steep lane of stubborn clay to the main road, I turned back for a last look. Was this because I sensed (as one often does) that something indoors was observing my departure? Then I noticed (what I had not registered before) a shapely shadow on the sill of an attic window: the once familiar outline of Horus the holy bird.

'How are you feeling?' I asked Jack now.

'Never better. In fact, I've got some very, very good news indeed. I didn't say anything about it before because I wanted to get this ghastly cure over and done with first. I've got a job! An extremely well-paid and – not to put too fine a point on it, as they say – really rather a grand and important job. That's why I took the cure – to make certain I'd be up to it.' Disarmingly pleased with himself, he struck an attitude. 'You are looking at the Middle East Correspondent of the *Sunday World*, no less! The paper with the biggest circulation in Fleet Street!'

Jack had had no previous experience of journalism, but had proved himself as a writer ten years earlier with a highly readable travel book, *Bulletin from Barbary*, about his adventures with nomadic tribesmen in North Africa. The *World's* Foreign Editor, a White's Club acquaintance of Jack's, had remembered this while looking for a suitable expert to cover the Arab–Israeli war and had commissioned him to contribute a series of special articles at an unusually high rate of payment. Jack's sympathies were fiercely pro-Arab; in political arguments he would often point out that anti-Zionism and anti-semitism were two quite separate things, implying (but never quite confirming) that in his case they did not co-exist. The proud male dignity of the Berber warriors had made a strong appeal to his aesthetic sense; he found in the wearing of loose robes a comfortable liberation from buttons, braces, collar studs and sock suspenders; and there was nothing in the subjection of women at odds with his own erotic tastes.

'I start in a fortnight! Just time to fit in a crash course in Arabic at the Berlitz school!' I began to congratulate him, but he cut me short. 'Which reminds me – I don't want to interfere – but isn't it about time for *you* to begin thinking about your future career? Everybody tells me that it's quite out of the question nowadays to keep oneself by writing – there's far too much competition and practically no demand. So you'd better put that idea right out of your head. If you don't feel cut out for the Diplomatic, or the Army, or the City, I couldn't understand more ... neither did I ... but I do believe that in modern socialist Britain it's essential to be *technically equipped* to earn your own living, to acquire some basic skill which is always going to be needed, whatever happens. Mightn't you perhaps take a *course* in something or other? I don't know what – glass-blowing, or something? Think about it, anyway. I know it's great fun sitting in the cinema all day but it doesn't really lead anywhere. Your mother's so sweet and I'm sure she'd be frightened of upsetting you so I thought I ought to speak to you instead . . . Look, I'm going to be late at the restaurant if we go on gassing like this, be an angel and pop downstairs and get them to order a cab for me, will you?'

A sacred place in Jack's life was reserved for his men friends. Furiously resented by his lovers, and humbly respected from a distance by his relations (who were seldom allowed to meet them), they represented a stabilising constant in his erratic emotional history. Most legendary of these – and in a sense the most mysterious – was Tony, a cheery little man who ran an art gallery in Mayfair. Tony had none of the obvious qualities (talent, wit, fame, wealth) which distinguished the other men friends and perhaps for this reason was ideally suited to fill the important role of confidential crony. It was from Tony that we heard the news of Jack's death. A sniper's bullet had hit him in the chest while he was incautiously standing without cover to take a photograph of a skirmish between Israeli troops and the Arab Legion: according to one rumour, he had been wearing Arab clothes at the time, but another eye witness reported that he had been dressed in khaki. Whatever the circumstances, this must have been that moment, which he had spent so much of his life dreading, when there just wasn't any wood around to touch. He had been working for the newspaper little more than a month; the Foreign Editor later forwarded a meagre parcel of personal belongings (a pocket diary, a cigarette lighter, an initialled handkerchief) but failed to recover his body; for reasons of diplomacy, the incident was played down in the Press.

My mother organised a memorial service for Jack at a Chelsea church. I sat next to his last girl, a streaky-haired beauty called Bobbie, who hadn't yet been properly taken in by the men friends and came as a shock to the longer-established mistresses. She cried miserably throughout the ceremony, incurring the disapproval of many in the congregation who seemed to feel that they had a greater right to grief but somehow lacked her facility in expressing it. Somebody gave an address about Jack, saluting him as an exemplar of the traditional British eccentric aristocrat with romantic leanings towards Islam: the names of Burton, Blunt and Lawrence were invoked. A theatrical clergyman read from Ecclesiastes: 'Also when they shall be afraid of that which is high, and fears shall be in the way, and the almond tree shall flourish, and the grasshopper shall be a burden, and desire shall fail: because man goeth to his long home ...' The words awoke suppressed, unwelcome memories of my father's funeral and I suddenly understood why Jack had been unable to face coming to that.

After the service, several of the mourners paused blinking in the porch to point out that, moving though it had been, there was no doubt that Jack would have preferred his friends to remember him by a *party*. 'With bags and bags of booze,' said Tony. Catching sight of me, he squeezed my arm. 'Just the chap I want to see ... Listen, so sorry, I should have told you sooner only there was a balls-up made by the solicitor.

Dear old Jack asked me to be his executor, you know, and he's mentioned you in his will. It seems he added a codicil at the last moment, just before he went off to the Middle East – says something about knowing that you'll understand what he means by it. Anyway, he's left you a sort of statue thing – not cash, I'm afraid, old boy, worse luck! I've got it for you at the gallery. Queer-looking object – not my period, so I've no idea what it would fetch. A hawk . . .'

I thought: 'It must never come back in the house – never.' That afternoon I called round at Tony's gallery, where an exhibition of paintings by Derain was being hung. The falcon was waiting for me in an office at the back. I raced with it to Spink's: my demeanour must have appeared both frantic and furtive, almost as though I suspected that I was being followed. The albino expert on Egyptian art was still there; did I only imagine that his smile of recognition suggested that he had been expecting my return for the past three years? I placed the god before him. He offered me a hundred pounds for it, which I happily accepted.

When I left the shop I was overwhelmed by an unfamiliar feeling of joy in which were mingled confidence, security and relief. It seemed to me certain that, by disposing of the falcon this second time, I had somehow managed to ward off the evil eye for ever. A curse had been lifted, a demon exorcised. I had a confused sense of triumph in having struck an easy bargain: it was as if I had been granted some unearned immunity, had been rewarded for doing nothing at all by a plenary indulgence. My mother and I would be safe now, for the rest of our lives ... But my mood of mysterious exaltation was accompanied by a nagging, trivial desire to understand the exact nature of the commercial transaction that had just taken place. The triple sale of the statuette contained a puzzling element, like those simple mathematical problems, Brain Twisters or Brain Teasers, which are sometimes used in IQ tests. What, in the matter of the ownership of Horus, had really happened? Had anything been materially gained, and if so, by whom? I had nearly reached Paddington before I had succeeded in working out the answer.

My mother and I had got rid of the falcon and had made two hundred pounds. Spink & Son Ltd had recovered the falcon and were ninety pounds down. Jack had lost both the falcon and a hundred and ten pounds. The six o'clock train had left the station, bearing me back home, and was passing Waterer's Floral Mile before I remembered that he had also lost his life.

Ursula

'Love worketh no ill to his neighbour;
therefore love is the fulfilling of the law.'

I

It was not long after Jack's death that I appeared in print for the first time. A friend of his, who had recently become the literary editor of a highbrow weekly, agreed to try me out as a novel-reviewer and published one short article over my name. If I had hoped for some reaction to this debut beyond my immediate circle, I was disappointed; but it would not be true to say that there was none at all. A few days later I was called to the telephone and addressed by an unfamiliar voice in clipped, confident and cultured tones.

'Fay Hitchcock here – remember me? Probably not, but I saw your stuff in the Staggers and the name rang a bell. My, my, we *have* grown up to be a clever young man, haven't we? Better watch out, though, if we get any sharper perhaps we'll cut ourselves one of these days! No, but *sans blague*, well done you, it was a remarkably able piece of work on the whole ... Look here, don't think me rude if I make it snappy, but I'm cooped up in this grim and ghastly bin – they call it a clinic but that's only window-dressing – and I'm far from being my own mistress, I can assure you. So listen, my real reason for calling is this: I thought you just might know – *what the dickens has happened to Bunch Bunbury*? I think something fishy's going on, I really do. I mean, can't the woman answer her own bloody telephone? My dear, I've rung and rung ...'

At this point, she was interrupted by an indistinct, yet audibly angry voice; there was the sound of an altercation succeeded by a scuffle, and then the line was disconnected. I was left with a troubled vision of poor Fay Hitchcock, having somehow managed to escape from the sinister vigilance of the *blouses blanches* to a telephone booth being discovered there, roughly apprehended and hauled back to a padded cell. The vision was by no means clear as I had only seen her once, very briefly, just before the war. I had a confused memory of crisp grey curls, flashing grey eyes, a diamond brooch on a grey tailor-made suit, the depressing scent of 'Tweed'. Where had it been? Of course – in none other than Bunch Bunbury's flat, to which I had been taken by my half-sister Ursula, who had been an intimate friend of them both in the roaring 'twenties.

When I wrote about my half-brother Jack, I never mentioned the fact that he had a full sister. This was not because Ursula was less important in my life. It is true that I saw much less of her – in fact, for reasons which will become apparent, I only met her on rare occasions – yet I always felt that I knew her the better of the two. He had indeed been a formidable presence throughout my childhood and adolescence, but she was to remain for ever significant by her absence: a domestic legend, partly scandalous and partly cosy, with the charm of a mystery that, given time, it should be perfectly possible to solve.

At first, all I knew was that in the autumn of 1929, when I was five and she was in her early thirties, Ursula had boarded one of the great trans-atlantic liners and set sail for the United States. I accompanied my parents to Southampton to see her off, but my only memory of the occasion is asking the name of a tune which the ship's orchestra was playing over and over again, and being told that it was called 'I'm a Dreamer – Aren't We All?' I think I must have expected Ursula to return after a short interval, but some time later I heard that instead of doing so she had decided to become an American citizen. I spent the next thirty-five years trying to imagine her life in New York.

In this attempt I was almost wholly unsuccessful. However, while still a child I found it easy to get some idea of what her life had been like up to the date of her departure, and to form a clear impression of her character and personality. My parents often spoke about her in my hearing. She was my father's adored only daughter, and he had observed her development since infancy with pride and amusement, preserving the recollection of significant occurrences during her girlhood in the ritualised – and subtly distorted – form of the family anecdote. She was also a close friend of my mother, who was only a few years older and had been her confidante during the early years of their maturity. My actual memory of Ursula grew increasingly vague throughout the decade that passed until I saw her again, and finally vanished altogether, having been replaced by a vicarious version of *their* memories – a vivid combination of second-hand knowledge and precocious intuition.

Photographs and paintings of Ursula as a little girl show a sturdy, stocky figure bundled into wide-collared Edwardian smocks and high button boots: brown hair, cut in a thick fringe and a shoulder-length bob, frames a round, beaming face. Her large grey eyes were her only beautiful feature, but the sweetness of her expression – suggesting an eagerness to please and the assumption of a similar generosity in other people – gave an effect of comeliness to her appearance as a whole.

From an early age she showed an extreme sensitivity to the sufferings (however slight and however brief) of other creatures, animal as well as human. That familiar nursery cry – 'It isn't *fair*!' – was often on her lips, but in Ursula's case it was uttered to draw attention, not to a grievance of her own, but to a suspected injustice visited on someone or something else. She was deeply upset by any manifestation of exclusion, of selectivity, of judgment – anything even faintly implying discrimination which (she had soon discovered) is likely to involve another person's feelings getting hurt; and, in so far as it lay within her power, she sought to prevent the expression of such tendencies in everybody with whom she came into contact. Her passionate commitment to total egalitarianism and unlimited tolerance inevitably landed her in the apparently contradictory position of exercising a certain moral authority; Ursula, whose affectionate nature made her popular with all her schoolfellows and won her many devoted 'best friends', was none the less seen by them as something of a bossy-boots.

Her family, too, while admiring her readiness to leap to the defence of any underdog, sometimes silently regretted that when Ursula brought a girl friend home with her she would almost invariably turn out to be unattractive or boring or maddening – and on occasion decidedly nasty; and that the slightest hint of even potential criticism of the guest would infuriate Ursula to a painful degree. Of course it was forbidden to laugh at these people, or indeed at any person whom she thought of as being disadvantaged, and this landed Ursula in yet another paradoxical situation, for she had a lively and spontaneous sense of the ridiculous and was often to be seen luxuriously incapacitated and lawlessly exalted by galvanic fits of the giggles. Unkindness made her ill; snobbery made her angry: once her eyes were seen to fill with tears and, when asked the reason, she explained that she had suddenly found herself thinking about little puppies being snubbed. After I was told of this incident many years later, I would lie awake at night worrying about Ursula lying awake at night worrying about sick and ill-treated animals ...

My father, a professional soldier, was often

abroad, and Ursula spent much of her childhood staying with his parents at Stars – a large, inconvenient house which they had made famous for an atmosphere of enlightened and eclectic hospitality. Here idealistic High Tory politics were underpinned by the Christian doctrine of all-embracing loving-kindness; reverence for art and beauty took the form of nostalgia for medieval romance and even contained a bracing element of Socialist principle (the interior of Stars had been designed by William Morris). One day, while Ursula and her grandparents were being driven back to the house after a visit to Salisbury Cathedral, their landau was intercepted by a dirty, drunken tramp who, muttering abuse, tried with some violence to enter it. The coachman knocked him aside with his whip, and speeded up the horses; but before they had time to move off Ursula opened the carriage door, leant out and with a gesture of courteous invitation said to the tramp: 'You are heartily welcome!'

Ursula was spared a conventional 'coming out season' by the outbreak of war in 1914. She worked for its duration as a VAD, finding in nursing the natural outlet for those qualities of dedication and enthusiasm which – considered handicaps in a young lady by the artificial standards of peacetime fashionable society – would have seriously impeded her success as a debutante. She found that she was happy: the horrors of pain and mutilation and death were to some extent exorcised by the fact that she was allowed to participate in the effort to relieve or prevent them. Her work ended when the war did – and Ursula had nothing to distract her from a full appreciation of its tragic depredations. Her brother Jack had been spared – but most of the young men she had known, or expected to know, were dead. She was fighting against a delayed depression when the Spanish influenza epidemic killed her mother; this seemed too much to bear, and Ursula suffered a brief collapse.

She recovered to find herself in a world that appeared to have got stuck while passing through some necessary stage of transition: as if temporarily stunned by the recent past, everything and everyone around her seemed tentative, indeterminate, incomplete and almost blank. The few suitable young men who had not only survived the war but were also prepared to act as Ursula's dancing partners were an uninspiring lot. She and her girl friends would refer to them as if they were horses who must not be overtaxed on the hunting field. 'I can't possibly go to this party tonight, I haven't got an escort.' 'Why not take So-and-So? He's quite presentable and perfectly safe.' 'Oh no, I couldn't do that, I had him out last week.' Exhausted by always having to take the initiative in the social-sexual game, and discouraged by the insignificant results with which her enterprise was rewarded, Ursula solemnly announced to Jack that she had made an important discovery: 'I really do believe that *all* men are impotent!'

Ursula and my mother (also a VAD) had made friends during the war. Both at loose ends, they now joined forces in what they admitted to be a rather feeble attempt to give themselves an occupation and perhaps even make a little money: they set themselves up as teachers of ballroom dancing. Among their few clients was an elderly, but up-to-the-minute, aunt of Ursula's, and my mother was leading this aunt round the floor in a foxtrot when my father shyly entered the room, curious to see how his daughter was getting on in her new venture. Soon after that first meeting between my parents the dancing lessons petered out – but there were more meetings, developing into courtship, engagement and ultimately marriage. Ursula was delighted to get her recently bereaved father 'off her hands' and into those of a trusted friend, and exhilarated to feel herself suddenly free of all family ties. She moved into a Chelsea studio with a young woman known as Flash Rumbold, where they worked together as portrait photographers: Ursula was responsible for the artistic posing of their subjects, revealing for this a remarkable flair, while Flash coped with those technical problems of lighting, time exposure and so on which Ursula, congenitally clumsy in practical matters, found beyond her.

Her association with Flash introduced Ursula to the wilder fringes of the post-war social phenomenon known to the Press as the Bright Young People, and with a sense of release that surprised her by its intensity she flung herself into an ardent exploration of every offered excess. A passionate admiration for the current idol of the 'gallery girls', Tallulah Bankhead, shared by Flash Rumbold, Bunch Bunbury, Fay Hitchcock and others in their group, made drunkenness seem glamorous to Ursula, while Brenda Dean Paul by her persuasively poised example led her on to experiment with heroin and cocaine. It must have seemed to her family and friends that Ursula was risking a troubled middle age and possibly an early death by indulging so wholeheartedly in these profitless dissipations; then, as the roaring 'twenties whimpered to a close, the course of her life dramatically changed direction. She fell in love.

Throughout the decade a series of revues with all-black casts (*Shuffle Along, Runnin' Wild, The Chocolate Dandies, Dixie to Broadway*) had been so popular with American audiences that some of them were brought over to Europe, where they were equally successful. By the spring of 1929, the *Blackbirds* company had reached the Moulin Rouge in Paris and was causing a sensation which it would later repeat in England. Meanwhile, a similar but more modest entertainment had opened in a 'little' London theatre. *Keep It Dark!* was not exactly a smash hit, but it attracted a discriminating and appreciative public who had made it, for a short while, the fashionable thing to see. Ursula was taken to *Keep It Dark!* by Flash Rumbold. The best thing in the show was a number called 'Mean Man', performed by a strikingly beautiful woman who was billed in the programme as 'Miss Ruby Richards'. The composer of 'Mean Man' had intended it to be a torch song, but Ruby Richards had made a reputation as a distinguished tragic actress rather than a *chanteuse*, and so instead of singing the tune she declaimed the lyrics, transforming them into a dramatic monologue – to such overwhelming effect that her curtain calls were greeted by hysterical cries of 'Bravo!', 'Bis!' and 'Encore!' Ursula and Flash went backstage to congratulate her: at that first meeting, Ursula was so moved that she could scarcely speak, but she returned to the theatre every night until the end of the limited run, after which it became necessary for Ruby to go back home to New York. A few months later, Ursula followed her out there. Ever since then, Ursula had lived with Ruby in the same small Harlem flat.

Most of her friends considered this latest exploit of Ursula's to be so extraordinary that it almost transcended scandal. For a 'well-brought-up' Englishwoman to vanish for good, apparently acting on a sudden whim, into a remote Negro ghetto confusedly associated in the ignorant British mind with drugs, drink, crimes of violence and embarrassing excesses of childish religious fervour ('Lordy, Lordy, Halleluiah!'), appeared to many of them a baffling enormity which, since it had no precedent, could hardly even be gossiped about; while the less narrow-minded, though applauding the courage and characteristic lack of caution manifested by her pioneer spirit, feared that she had taken a final step into unexplored territory where it would be too dangerous for them to follow. Whether they thought of her as a social outcast who had wandered off for ever beyond the pale, or as an exiled heroine, a 'Queen over the water' who might some day return to her faithful people, for them all Ursula had been transmogrified into a 'lost lady' of legend.

2

When I was old enough to take a little of all this in, it struck me as a fascinatingly romantic story. I became obsessed by the need to understand it more clearly and felt perpetually teased by a sense of unsatisfied curiosity. Harlem! What on earth could it be like? To a schoolboy during the 1930s the name meant only one thing: jazz. This was puzzling, because I could make no connection between my memories of Ursula and that exciting, grown-up yet frowned-upon form of music. My mother was among the first English subscribers to the *New Yorker*, and I would spend hours studying the section at the beginning of the magazine devoted to night spots, supper clubs, jazz cellars and cabaret 'rooms', vainly trying to imagine the aunt-like figure of Ursula sitting in one of these (I had only a few Hollywood musicals to go by in my attempt to recreate the scene and the decor was maddeningly hazy) while Maxine Sullivan swung 'Loch Lomond' or Ethel Waters shouted the blues. There was always something basically improbable about these visions: Ursula remained Ursula and Harlem remained Harlem, and even though I knew that the two had somehow achieved a synthesis in the outside world, they were still thesis and antithesis to my private mind.

My mother shared to some extent my unbridled interest in the matter and blatant desire for further detail, while also participating in my father's indulgent and unquestioning acceptance of the whole eccentric episode as 'typical of darling Ursie'. I could tell that the more distant members of the family pitied him almost as if he had been the victim of some hideous outrage, but he deflected their patronising approaches to condolence by refusing to recognise any cause for it. He had inherited from his own mother and father their stern gospel of love: 'I do not mind what my children do, so long as they are happy.' (This gospel is not in effect quite so unrestrainedly libertarian as it seems, for it not only enjoins happiness on one as a duty but also carries with it the inhibiting implication that whatever one might do must automatically be right merely because one is a child of the speaker – and any act of defiance, experiment or destruction is thus rendered meaningless before it has been committed.)

Although Ursula and my parents hardly ever wrote to each other there was no real question of their having 'lost touch'; rather, their intimacy was felt to exist at a deeper level than the plane of formal social intercourse to which letters (other than love letters) belong, and indeed the few that did pass between them exuded an apologetic air of irrelevance. It was as if they sensed that a regular correspondence would have emphasised their separation more than it could have relieved it: instead they decided, as it were politely, to ignore it. Any important piece of news would be transmitted by cablegram, or in urgent cases by telephone: I remember the excitement of waiting for the insecure transatlantic connection and the sense of reassurance conveyed by Ursula's husky voice, faint but sturdily confidential, when it eventually reached us over the humming, crackling line. At Christmas she would send me flatteringly adult presents (*John Brown's Body* by Stephen Vincent Benét, *Will Shakespeare* by Clemence Dane) accompanied by notes as brief as they were affectionate. For concrete information about Ursula and her surroundings, we were almost totally dependent on Hope Barker and her annual visits to 'scout' for English books which might be suitable for publication by her husband's New York firm.

Ursula and Hope had been fellow pupils at a boarding school for the daughters of Army officers, and had later worked together as VADs in the same hospital near Rouen: it was there that my mother had met them both, and the three high-spirited young women had become for a time inseparable. After the Armistice, their lives had taken different directions; but when Ursula first set foot on Manhattan to take up residence in Harlem, Hope had been for some years installed with her American husband in a duplex apartment on Beekman Place, and their former friendship was happily revived. Hope had taken no part in the *louche* life led by Ursula in London during the 1920s, and was herself irreproachably respectable; the conventional New York 'set' to which she belonged was far removed from the less privileged milieu so impulsively embraced by Ursula; and yet Hope was to remain Ursula's most loyal ally. She prided herself on the broadness and openness of her mind, and often said that the only thing that shocked her was the assumption by others that she had been shocked. With mock fury and conscious comedy, she would deliver herself of the cliché:

'I'm afraid it would take a great deal more than that to shock *me*!'

Yes, Hope Barker was a woman of the world: her manner proclaimed it as a salient fact. This manner had presumably been developed as a badge of superiority during periods of her life which had been spent among people to whom the phrase could not have applied (her contemporaries at the hunt balls and gymkhanas of her girlhood, the majority of her colleagues while nursing during the war), but even after her marriage to a successful publisher, when she moved in circles sophisticated enough to make the reminder unnecessary, it continued to be insisted upon. This was partly achieved by an air of immense, if slightly mysterious, authority; she gave the impression of being somehow special, a person of unusually wide experience whose words, pronounced with dramatic emphasis and charged with tolerant humour, carried peculiar weight. People meeting her for the first time found themselves after a while uneasily wondering why they had never heard about her before and sensing something shameful in their ignorance. Later, they would try to become better informed: was she perhaps a famous character actress? a distinguished novelist? a 'personality' of some kind or another? But Hope was none of these, nor did she wish to be; serenely secure in her comparative obscurity, she needed no vulgar testimonial of achievement to justify her superb self-confidence.

She would arrive to stay with my mother with some of the glamour of luxury shipboard travel still clinging to her, although she did not belong to a physically glamorous type. (One of her favourite stories was about her nephew who, asked to give a description of her appearance when she had somehow got lost going through Customs at Southampton, replied: 'My aunt could be said to possess the unique distinction of striking a happy medium between Claudette Colbert and Harpo Marx!') As soon as she had settled herself in the house, my mother and I would put her through an avid third degree: this produced some intriguing glimpses into Ursula's way of life, but (as when overzealous interrogators find that their victim has fainted under torture) we were always ultimately frustrated in our thirst to possess a fuller picture.

'Do you see her often?'

'Not as often as I should like, alas. I don't think you people over here can fully comprehend the barbaric customs still in force in the so-called Land of the Free, but a ludicrous and abominable thing exists there called the *colour bar* – officially in the South, unofficially but none the less effectively in the North. It is just conceivable that if Ruby paid a call on me, the porter of the apartment building where I live might consider himself justified in requesting her to use the tradesmen's lift at the rear entrance. Ruby therefore quite rightly refuses to come and visit me, and darling Ursie naturally wouldn't dream of coming on her own, although Ruby has *begged* her to do so, literally on bended knee, time and time again ... but you know how fiercely loyal Ursie is, and she also feels that she would be somehow giving countenance to the detestable system if she didn't take a stand. All of which needless to say I couldn't agree with more.

So *I* go to *them* whenever I can – but I'm a busy woman and, as I say, it isn't *nearly* as often as I would wish.'

'Do they have a nice flat?'

'It depends what you mean by "nice". There's certainly nothing nasty about it. Quite simply furnished – apart from a few pieces which Ursie has clung on to from the old days at Stars, family pictures, some decent china, that kind of thing. It's too touching the way, ever since she's been living in Harlem, Ursie has become more and more of the county lady – which, God knows, she never used to be over here! Their apartment is probably the only place in the whole of the United States where one is offered Earl Grey tea, cucumber sandwiches and Gentleman's Relish!'

'What is Ruby *like*?'

'Simply delightful. A woman of enormous magnetism, great personal distinction, and knock-down charm!'

'Do describe her!'

'Describe Ruby?' Hope reflected. 'Not easy... You see, there's something very special about her that's almost impossible to put into words. To begin with, she has the most tremendous dignity. I mean, if she were to walk into the room at this moment, you'd say to yourself: *who* is that fascinating creature? It's not so much that she's pretty or elegant or what-have-you – but she just does happen to have been born with this extraordinary *presence*. And such warmth! I think she's probably the warmest person I've ever come across. Take it from me, Ruby Richards is a very remarkable human being indeed. Everybody I've met who knows her agrees that she's quite, quite wonderful. They're all bowled over. So would you be.'

'What does she *look* like?'

'Striking, I'd say – in the Spanish style. In fact, you'd swear she was Spanish if you knew nothing to the contrary. People often do take her for a Latin American or a Mediterranean. But of course she's much too proud to "pass as white". To be perfectly honest, it would have been better for her if she had, from the point of view of her career. She's a highly gifted actress, but she's always refused to play maids, or slaves, or any form of caricatured "coon", and those are almost the only parts offered to Negroes on the Broadway stage. So she's hardly ever *in* anything – which is a scandalous waste of talent. But all the same she's regarded with the highest respect by her fellow artistes. I can vouch for that. Kit Cornell herself told me that Ruby's timing was impeccable. Impeccable!'

'What sort of life do they lead? Who do they see?'

'Well, Ruby has a fairly large circle of extremely interesting and worthwhile friends – actors, singers, writers, artists of all sorts, as well as people seriously dedicated to furthering the Negro cause. But I'm afraid she does find dear Ursie's total lack of discrimination just a fraction trying at times! You know how our angel has never been able to bear the *thought* of anybody being left out of things or made to feel the slightest bit inferior – and if she had her way, my dear, she'd fill the place with the sweepings of the Harlem streets: drug fiends, pimps, prostitutes of *both* sexes! It's too hard on poor Ruby, who has spent years struggling to establish a very highly regarded *salon* in order to scotch the purely sordid image of Harlem which prejudiced outsiders assume to be the norm.'

'How does Ursula go down with Ruby's friends?'

'Oh, I think they all adore her – though, as I say, some of them feel desperately sorry for Ruby when Ursie's lovely unsnobbishness gets out of hand and she gives the unfortunate impression of liking *anybody* just so long as they're black! There are naturally just as many subtle shades of social distinction in Harlem as in any other community, and I think discovering this came as rather a shock to Ursie, who of course has always loathed that sort of thing and had hoped to get clean away from it. But on the whole I'm sure they do appreciate her throwing in her lot with them as the beautiful gesture it undoubtedly is. I think in the end she even won over Spencer, though it wasn't easy at first.'

'Who on earth is Spencer?'

'Ruby's husband,' Hope replied calmly.

'*What*?'

'Oh, yes. They were married practically in the cradle, I believe, and it's been what is politely referred to as a "union in name only" for years. I nearly', said Hope wittily, 'called it a *mariage blanc* – but that wouldn't be quite the *mot juste*, would it? However – be that as it may, as they say – Ruby is utterly devoted to Spencer and won't *hear* of his being kicked out of the apartment. So he lives there with them. He's perfectly harmless – a charming good-for-nothing. Refuses to do a hand's turn, but it's hard not to like him. You know, the sort of person one talks about having a "soft spot" for.'

Gradually, some sort of blurred impression was emerging from Hope's brisk and bracing commentary: a small but otherwise featureless flat; Spencer hanging about in it all day long doing nothing; Ruby unable to find suitable employment as an actress but valiantly, and with her habitual dignity, persevering as a *salonnière*; Ursula an exotic, ungainly presence among them, accepted (with a touch of condescension) as an equal by their social circle in spite of the fact that she sometimes made a nuisance of herself – either by assuming the stuck-up airs of an English gentlewoman or by tactlessly insisting on opening their doors to the scum of the earth.

'Is she happy?'

'Blissfully. She worships Ruby, and asks nothing better from life than to be allowed to be near her. Also, she has found the perfect outlet for her crusading instincts and reforming zeal in the Negro cause – into which she has wholeheartedly thrown herself.'

It appeared, however, that even Ursula's selfless commitment to this had involved Ruby in some embarrassment. Hope told us about the case of the Scottsboro Boys, and tried to explain the split among their defenders between the moderate National Association for the Advancement of Colored People and the radical International Labor Defense. 'Ursie has been influenced by her old friend Nancy Cunard into unqualified support for the revolutionary ILD, which violently attacks the liberal NAACP and its magazine *Crisis* as bourgeois and reactionary – you know, the fashionable Communist jargon (not that Ursie is a Communist *herself*, I'm sure) – which is a *tiny* bit awkward as *Crisis* happens to be edited by the great Negro leader Dr Du Bois, who needless to say is one of Ruby's most valued – nay, *treasured* acquaintances! But Ruby takes it in her stride. "I rise above it," she says. At the moment Ursie is very busy helping a friend with research for some scholarly work in several volumes on the history of the American Negro. It's quite a humble job she's got, but an extremely demanding one, and she works at it like a – help! there I go again – not like a black, perish the thought – like a *horse*!'

It was this job that eventually brought Ursula back to us (her researches having led her to the British Museum and the Public Record Office), on a visit as transient as one of Persephone's, in the spring of 1939.

3

I missed her arrival as I was away at school but when I came home for the summer holidays I found her established in the house as harmoniously as if she had always lived there. She was to spend her weekends with us in the country and the rest of the time working in London, where she had various friends who could put her up. I think her appearance must have come as something of a surprise to me at first – perhaps even a shock – but in less than a day her physical presence had acquired a comfortable aura of familiarity, as if some homely and haphazard miracle had released a deeply buried folk memory and clumsily made it flesh.

Ursula, not much more than forty, looked years older. Her face had no more lines on it than was natural at her age but she made no attempt to conceal them apart from a vague sprinkling of powder. Her hair had become colourless and thin; when out of doors, she covered it with an extremely dowdy hat designed in the shape of a mushroom from scraps of grey felt and black satin. This hat (also sometimes sprinkled with face powder) appeared to have a squashy, almost squelchy consistency. Her manner was the reverse of effusive: dry, reserved, slightly governessy in tone, as if in dread of sentimental gush. It was clear that she was still very shy. She had a graceless, rather knock-kneed walk, which was none the less appealing in its suggestion of impetuous haste and eager welcome. Extremely short-sighted, she was constantly bumping into, knocking over or treading on things that had been placed in her path. This had made her devotedly dependent on a pair of spectacles with pale tortoise-shell frames – and not only as an aid to vision. If one was about to tell Ursula a piece of news which she expected to interest or entertain her, she would cry: 'Wait a moment – *do* wait till I've found my glasses – you know I can't enjoy anything properly without them!' Then, spectacles on nose, she would turn to one a sweet, serious face in cosy complicity and confident anticipation of pleasure.

Ursula was worried about a book she had been sent. It was called '*Crinkum-Crankum* and other poems by Enid ffrench', and had been privately printed on a hand-worked press by a 'vanity' publishing firm in Eastbourne. Enid ffrench was a friend from the past: with shingled hair, a trim figure and a *gamine* face, she had been fairly well known playing supporting roles on the London stage during the 1920s, usually cast as a slangy Bright Young Thing in some starring vehicle for Lilian Braithwaite, Gladys Cooper or Fay Compton. (This I knew from drawings of her illustrating theatre reviews which I would sometimes come across in old bound volumes of *Punch*.) Then she had suddenly disappeared from view. Ursula had heard a rumour that she had become a nun, but apparently this was false. She had written an affectionate inscription on the flyleaf of *Crinkum-Crankum*, begging Ursula to tell her what she thought of the book ('I know you'll be truthful – you always were') and giving her present address in a Sussex nursing home.

'What on earth am I to put in my letter?' said Ursula. 'Normally the technique in this sort of tricky situation is to find *one thing* to praise in a friend's book and concentrate on that for several pages, but the fact is I can't discover a single line in these poems which I can honestly admire! It really is a poser. There's no point in faking it, either, the old girl's much too shrewd to be fooled by that. On the other hand I really *must* think of something kind to say to her. It looks as if she's been having a pretty thin time of it, poor darling.'

The poems in *Crinkum-Crankum* were indeed

very bad, but none the less I found them fascinating. One in particular, called 'Gardening', had an opening line which haunted me – and which I still remember: 'I hang my woollie on a branch.' There was something so feeble about this line that I became quite intoxicated by bewilderment at the thought that anybody (even if only the author) had presumed to call it 'poetry'. At the same time, the image of the woollie hanging on the branch did succeed in suggesting another, almost as vivid, of Enid ffrench's neat figure squatting near by, her shingled head shielded by a floppy sunhat and bent over the border she was weeding ... If it could do that, surely it must be 'poetry' after all? I said some of this to Ursula, who listened intently. 'Thank you, darling, you've saved my bacon!' She eventually sent off a long, loving letter to Enid ffrench, with an appreciation of her book so attentive to minor detail that the vagueness of the general verdict was effectively concealed, and finishing with a postscript: 'My young brother has been absorbed by "C-C" as well and asks me to tell you that he *particularly* revels in the one about your garden.'

One Friday evening, Ursula brought her former partner, Flash Rumbold, down to stay, warning us beforehand that she had recently dropped the nickname and wished to be known as Fleur. She was now an extremely successful photographer, with premises in Mayfair and a reputation for social portraiture rivalling those of Harlip and Yevonde. Fleur was tall and slender and ultra-feminine, with frizzy fair hair, round blue eyes and a round red mouth: her features appeared to have been nervously dabbed on her face just a little askew, as in a painting by Marie Laurencin. She wore expensive clothes made of soft materials in pastel shades – 'I'm model size, you see', she would explain, lowering turquoise-tinted lids. In spite of a manner of speaking so affected as to induce symptoms of dissociation in her listeners, Fleur did exert a certain languid glamour: it soon became clear, however, that her egocentricity bordered on the monstrous.

After dinner on Sunday somebody – probably Fleur – suggested a seance. A round table with a slippery surface was produced; a wine glass was placed upside down in the centre and the cards of a 'Lexicon' pack arranged in a circle along the edge. My father did not take part – remembering all too clearly the sad vogue for spiritualism after the last war, when so many of his bereaved relations had been driven for consolation to mediums whom, in less stricken circumstances, they would have immediately recognised as blatantly fraudulent. Fleur, Ursula, my mother and myself sat at the table and each lightly rested a finger on the glass.

We asked questions about the crisis in Europe – would there be war, and if so, when? – but the glass made no movement more decisive than a tremulous wobble. 'We're being too serious, I expect,' said Ursula. 'Perhaps we ought to start with a lighter topic.' For a while none of us could think of anything suitable to say. Then Ursula politely inquired whether Fleur would enjoy her projected holiday at Rapallo, about which we had already heard a good deal, and the glass hastened to spell out a definite YES. Further questions pertaining to Fleur and her affairs were received in the same positive spirit; but the glass appeared to be bored by any other subject, responding either with a stubborn refusal to budge or at best with a listless stagger towards letters which were impossible to form into any recognisable word.

It seemed to me obvious that Fleur was directing the glass herself, but this simple solution to the frustrating mystery did not occur to Ursula, who soon began to bully the 'control' which she assumed to be animating the wine glass. 'Go away!' she told it rudely. 'You're a nasty unclean spirit and we don't want you here. Go away at once and send a nice clean spirit in your place.' I noticed that Ursula was taking a much tougher tone with the wine glass than one could ever imagine her adopting towards a mortal being.

Finally the spirit surlily intimated that it was unable to co-operate until the doubter among us had been banished from the room. This could only refer to me. Terrified that I might be offended, Ursula insisted on calling the seance off, while Fleur gazed reproachfully at the mirror in her powder compact. I assured Ursula that I would be happy to sit in my father's study next door and read. 'It might be safer if he were on a different floor altogether,' said Fleur. 'I've always heard that hostile vibrations are more likely to carry horizontally than vertically.' In spite of the look of innocent distress on Ursula's face, I obediently said goodnight and went upstairs to bed.

The following morning I travelled up with Ursula by train to London, where I had an appointment with my dentist. Fleur, who had come by car, stayed behind before driving off a little later to visit friends in the West Country. Once alone with Ursula in the railway carriage, I could not resist telling her of my suspicions regarding the seance. 'Do you really think she was cheating?' she asked, surprised but only mildly so. Then she laughed. 'How *very* funny! I must say, the joke's on me – fancy my not spotting it! I'm sure you're right, but I think she deserves the benefit of the doubt and I'm going to try to keep this just between ourselves . . . though I must say it does make an awfully good story and I shall probably succumb to temptation.'

Ursula and I then talked for the first time about politics. She told me how exhilarated she had felt on leaving England for a society where the old class barriers no longer applied, and how swiftly she had been made aware of the yet graver injustice of racial prejudice; but she insisted that her experience as an immigrant had not been one of disillusion. Indeed, she spoke of America – and in particular of Franklin and Eleanor Roosevelt – with possessive patriotic pride. At the same time, she retained a vestigial allegiance to the old regime. She had bitterly resented the Abdication as an insult to American womanhood, and was still romantic about the Duke of Windsor: 'He will always be the true King of England as far as *I'm* concerned!' She described her present dilemma as a confirmed pacifist whose hatred of Nazism was so great that she sometimes found herself hoping for war. 'Do you know that horrible feeling of being just like a chameleon on a plaid? One hardly knows any longer *what* one thinks or what one wants to happen. I remember I first had it years ago when I decided the only thing to do was to become a vegetarian and then didn't go through with it as I still had to buy meat to give to my darling dogs and cats! But this of course is far grimmer. I can't *bear* the thought of the slaughter that another war would be bound to bring about ... but then if the whole of Europe goes Fascist, *that* would be too hideous to contemplate as well!'

Ursula was staying at a flat in Wigmore Street belonging to her friend Bunch Bunbury, and on arrival at Paddington we took a taxi there. 'Do come in for a moment if you've got time before your appointment. I'm longing to show you off to more of my friends and I think you'll enjoy Bunch – she's got a first-class brain. There may', she added tentatively, 'be somebody there called Fay Hitchcock who can be rather difficult, but she's very nice really. Just so long as she's not in a funny mood ...' Ursula had a key to the flat, which admitted us into a long, dark passage with what appeared to me to be a great many doors leading off it, as in a hotel corridor. There was a strong scent of 'Tweed' and we seemed to be following it like police dogs to its source in a small drawing-room at the back, where we found Fay Hitchcock sitting morosely alone. After she had introduced us, Ursula asked: 'Where's Bunch?'

'Search me,' said Fay shortly, and then began to question me in a matey way about my life at school. 'Are you a wet bob or a dry bob, old boy?' On hearing that I was a dry bob she tried to get a discussion going about cricket, but this was a subject that bored me and soon my uninspired response started to irritate her. 'If you're not keen on games I suppose you must be artistic. What did you think of the Academy this year? Pretty good rubbish, wasn't it?' For a second I was tempted to bluff, but sensing that Fay would be hard to deceive I confessed that I had never been to Burlington House.

She turned in exasperation to Ursula. 'What the devil *does* this brother of yours take an interest in, for Pete's sake? God, how I hate indifference – especially in the young! Youth should be a time of passion, of bold adventure, of wholehearted commitment ... If there is one thing I *cannot* stand, it is caution! There's nothing worse, in my humble opinion, than lukewarm lack of enthusiasm. I really don't care what people are enthusiastic about, just so long as they're enthusiastic about *something*! Better to feel strongly about anything than nothing at all! If you ask me, it's lack of enthusiasm which has got this world of ours into the stinking mess that it's in today!'

Fay was interrupted by the sound of the flat door opening; she stopped her tirade and furiously lit a cigarette. Bunch came into the room: a large, dark, brooding presence, she stood for a moment in dramatic silence, staring at the floor. I had time to notice that she wore a broad belt of shiny black patent leather and was carrying an outsize handbag of the same material: both belt and bag were studded by chips of coloured glass to form a pattern suggesting the night sky. Then she planked the bag down on a table, slightly displacing a framed photograph by Cecil Beaton of Ursula dressed in a French fisherman's striped jersey and a sailor's bell-bottom trousers.

'Well – you may congratulate me,' Bunch announced. 'I have just landed my first job. I think a little drinky-poo is called for, *non*?' She poured herself a whisky and soda, gesturing to the rest of us to help ourselves. After a long swig, she murmured: 'That's better. I needed that.'

Fay continued to sulk, but Ursula was generously excited by Bunch's news. I gathered from their questions and replies that the job was with a famous department store in Oxford Street and had something to do with the belt and the handbag, which she had designed herself. 'They want me to do more stuff for them in the same line, and if it goes down all right they might take me on as a buyer as well – for my sins! But at least it means the gas bill will be paid!'

After this the conversation became more enjoyable from my point of view, turning to films and the stage. Bunch was an expert on the French cinema, and told me that Arletty was a chum of hers 'in real life'. Fay declared that she was just about to join a theatre club which planned to produce works refused a licence by the British censor – 'Things like Lillian Hellman's *The Children's Hour*.' Ursula, who had seen this on Broadway, said that she thought it rather a silly play.

I left Ursula in the flat and walked to the dentist's in a state of moderate over-excitement; then I saw a film at the Curzon cinema which had been recommended by Bunch and took a train back home. That evening I noticed that my mother seemed preoccupied and a few days later she told me why. Before her departure, Fleur Rumbold had insisted on their having a private talk: apparently she was very concerned about Ursula. According to Fleur, a main reason for Ursula's visit to England had been to seek a cure for heroin addiction. She had been introduced to the drug in the wild old days at the Chelsea studio, and life in Harlem had offered irresistible opportunities to increase her dependence. Somebody had told her of a man in Harley Street with a wonderful new treatment and she had come over to consult him ... 'I just thought her family ought to know,' Fleur had finished.

'I really shouldn't involve you in this,' my mother said now, 'but that awful woman upset me so much that I had to tell somebody. Whatever happens, Yvo must never get to hear of it: the worry would be so terribly dangerous for his health.' My father had suffered a severe heart attack the previous winter, and my mother was desperate to spare him anxiety.

But Ursula never underwent the cure; for the second time she was rescued from an impending ordeal by the outbreak of war. Her loyalties were painfully divided: she felt that she should stay in the land of her birth to share its danger, but she knew that she would return to her adopted country to be with Ruby. For a week or so she immersed herself in war work, helping at railway stations to deal with the problems of premature panic evacuation from London, and then she went back to New York. I was at school when she left, and unable to say goodbye. Another twenty years were to pass before I saw her again.

4

'She'll never come over,' Hope Barker reported decisively. 'Since her father's death, followed so tragically soon by Jack's, she has felt that England would be too full of sad associations. I honestly believe that she couldn't bear to see it again.'

This was in 1950. Hope's transatlantic trips had started up once more after a hiatus imposed by the war and prolonged by unexplained domestic complications. My mother and I had recently moved to a small house in Knightsbridge where she let rooms to young men from South American embassies while I worked fitfully as a freelance literary journalist. It almost seemed to us now that Hope didn't *want* Ursula to make a reappearance in our midst, as if such an event might undermine her authority as our sole source of news and weaken the impact of her artistically spaced revelations.

We already knew from Ursula herself that, as soon as America entered the war, she had enlisted as a private in the WACs. From Fleur we had heard that the stimulus of this challenge had enabled her to rid herself for ever of the heroin habit. Ursula had served with distinction as an Army photographer, ending up with the rank of sergeant. It so happened that she was the first WAC to set foot on Australian soil, and a blurred snapshot of her doing so was widely syndicated in the American Press. Another news photograph from that period had reached us: Ursula, beaming in khaki, stood between a nervous-looking young man in civilian clothes and an imposing lady, with a smile like Mrs Roosevelt's, dressed in a colonel's uniform. A caption explained that Ursula was introducing a distant cousin of hers, who was a member of the household of the Governor of New South Wales, to the Commanding Officer of the WACs in the South-West Pacific Area.

We now learned from Hope that, after demobilisation from the Army, Ursula had taken a post working for a government department in charge of the welfare of war veterans. 'She's absolutely wonderful about it, gets up at crack of dawn every single day of the week and struggles to the office by bus and the subway, which I can assure you is no picnic. The job isn't tremendously well paid but it carries certain privileges with it and she'll have quite a nice pension when she reaches retirement age – if she can only stick it out that long, which she is determined to do. I think she gets a big kick out of being the breadwinner – you know, very much the man of the family, coming home exhausted every evening to find Ruby waiting.'

In spite of this, Hope considered that it was really Ruby who looked after Ursula, rather than the other way round. 'I wish I had a dollar', she said impressively, 'for every time that Ruby has poured out to me her desperate worry that there would be nobody to take care of Ursula should anything happen to *her*. "The truth of the matter is, Hope," I remember her saying, "that I *dare* not be the first to go! I can't stand the thought of what would become of my darling. I've just got to keep on living – whether I like it or not – because, quite simply, I'm too scared to die!"'

'But why should she die?'

'Oh, she's what is known as "getting on", you know. Ruby is at least ten years older than Ursula, though she looks years younger. She's not going to live for ever.'

'And what exactly is she afraid will happen to Ursula when she does die?'

Hope explained that, although it was true that Ursula had with considerable heroism given up drugs completely, her past indulgence had left her in superficially good health while damaging her brain to a degree where even the slightest sip of alcohol would make her as intoxicated as if she had been on a bender. 'Ruby has to be constantly on the lookout that not one drop passes her lips. I mean, if there's sherry in the trifle ... *fatal*, my dear! And of course Ursula wouldn't take that sort of supervision from anybody else but Ruby, who knows how to be both tactful and firm. "For *my* sake, sweetheart," she says: and Ursula pulls herself together at once.'

'How does it affect her when she does get drunk? Is she violent, or what?'

'No, no, nothing like that. She just gets – well, *silly*. It's agony for Ruby to have to sit by while Ursie lets herself down by behaving – I can't offhand think of another word – in a thoroughly *silly* way.'

But on her next visit, Hope brought better news: Ruby had at last been offered – and had accepted – a role in a play that was almost worthy of her talent. It was a turgid poetic melodrama called *Twenty-Eight Young Men Bathe by the Shore*, set in Acapulco and dealing with murder, incest, homosexuality and witchcraft. Ruby played a Mexican peasant woman who crosses the stage at a crucial moment in the plot and utters a weird prophetic warning, something between a blessing and a curse. 'It's the *tiniest* part, but my God, does she make the most of it!' said Hope. 'She called me before opening night and said "Don't sneeze, darling, or you'll miss me altogether!" but she needn't have worried. The way she delivers that single line sends shivers down one's spine – *electrifying*! *Young Men* is *the* smash hit on Broadway at the moment – what they call over there "the hottest ticket in town" – and the critics to a man have given it rave reviews. Quite a few of them mentioned Ruby. It's most gratifying that after all this time she's getting something approaching her due. Ursie of course is as proud as Punch.'

I felt that I would have given anything to see Ruby in that play. Throughout the 1940s and the 1950s, America was the place above all others where I longed to be. My favourite films, my favourite singers, many of my favourite writers came from there. In spite of repeated warnings not to do so, I persisted in the pardonable error of identifying America with Hollywood and New York. The idea that so close a relation as Ursula actually lived in one of these glamorous cities was constantly thrilling and increasingly tantalising as, year after year, I failed to find an adequate excuse to justify the expense of the journey. I naïvely wrote to ask her if she had ever met Lena Horne, and she replied: 'No, sorry, I don't know your pin-up girl, but Ruby knows Hazel Scott's husband, if that's any good! The Rev. Adam Clayton Powell Jr – a truly remarkable person and the first Negro Congressman in New York ... Sadie sends wishes, says she appreciated your gracious hospitality but complains that she thought it rather ungallant of you to refuse to escort her round the night-spots! What went wrong?!'

Sadie was one of the stream of people sent over by Ursula with letters of introduction to my mother. It must be said that these visitors nearly always turned out a cruel disappointment. Instead of Lena Horne or Adam Clayton Powell, we got ... well, for example, Sadie. The remarkable thing about her was that she was a judge, though we found this difficult to believe. A well-preserved white woman in her fifties, she arrived at our house early one afternoon and announced that she was coming back later to cook dinner for us. She gave us a list of the ingredients she would need, of which the main one was wild rice – at that time almost impossible to obtain in London. She also said that she expected me to 'squire' her round all the fashionable nightclubs ('and maybe a few honky-tonks as well!'), making it clear that the bills would be taken care of by herself. Sadie then left, to shop around for a sexy, slinky evening dress.

My mother set out on a frantic, unsuccessful search for wild rice, while I made a panic-stricken attempt to discover if any nightclub might be persuaded to admit two non-members. Sadie returned as promised, triumphantly smoothing the sexy, slinky dress over her hips, and almost immediately got aggressively drunk. The dinner was never cooked, and Sadie was clearly in no fit state to go dancing – although she did not see it that way herself. I finally took her in a taxi back to her hotel, which she was only persuaded to enter after an embarrassing scene, the details of which I soon afterwards contrived to forget. Ever since this incident, I find that the phrase 'sober as a judge' can reawaken a throbbing consciousness of my humiliating social ineptitude.

Shortly after Sadie's visit I got a job in publishing, and for a delusive moment in the mid-1950s it looked as if this might provide a pretext for visiting the United States: incontinently, I wrote to Ursula announcing my imminent arrival, but the whole plan had collapsed before I received her reply. 'I am so excited and delighted', she wrote, 'to think that I am going to see you again after such a long, long time. It seems to me that last time I saw you you were a public schoolboy but rather a grand and grown-up one and now you are a distinguished man. "Well I never," as our Nannies used to say. As you see from above address, we now live in Brooklyn – what a pity that you never saw the old Harlem place! I wish you could stay with us, we have a lovely room for you with paintings of Jack and Father from Stars, but unfortunately it would not be convenient for you for business appointments. It is now a complete slum since the City took it over but the house is still nice and representative of what houses used to be like before the "City Fathers" determined that we should all live in little box-like apartments. I think we will have to move to the suburbs. You being the head of the family I will probably bore you considerably asking your advice on this. Are you a good businessman? At the moment I am very overworked which is why I did not answer your letter by return. The house is full of puppies but Ruby who wants to add a note will tell you all the home news as I must get off to work.'

Ruby's note read: 'Cheers! I never for a moment doubted that one day you would get to N.Y. Naturally you will be very busy, yet I hope we will see a lot of you. On the other hand, there is so much to see, such a variety of things you will want to do, in this unique conglomerate city, that I would not want you to miss a bit of it. Meanwhile, do remember what a warm welcome will always await you.'

'Ursie was heartbroken that you couldn't make it after all,' said Hope when I saw her next. My mother asked her if she knew what had prompted the move to Brooklyn.

'A number of factors, the principal one I believe being the death of Spencer, which severed Ruby's last real link with Harlem. For some time both she and Ursie had been pining for a home where the atmosphere would be a little more *gemütlich*.'

Mention of Ruby's husband – for us a figure as shadowy as a minor character in a novel one has never read – reminded my mother of an even vaguer masculine image from an imperfectly realised episode in the whispered past. 'Wasn't there once, ages ago, some talk of *Ursula* being married – or, at any rate, engaged? I seem to remember Yvo getting letters about it, and saying it sounded like a good thing, and then suddenly telling me that nothing had come of it and it would be better if the subject was never mentioned again.'

Hope looked grave. 'That, my darling, was typical of your saintly husband. He was determined to shield you from any unpleasantness – and he clearly succeeded in doing so.' I remembered how determined my mother had been to shield my father from knowledge of Ursula's drug addiction – and how she too had apparently succeeded in her aim.

'What *are* you talking about, Hope darling?'

Hope's instinct for drama stood her now in better stead than (so far as we were concerned) it ever had or ever would. She managed to guy its expression without diminishing its effect. 'My lips, as they say, have been sealed hitherto – but so many bridges have gone under the water since then (to coin a cliché!) that I see no reason why you shouldn't hear about it now, so here goes. *Well* ... a year or so after Ursula's arrival in New York, she became involved with this deeply deplorable creature. He went by the name of Morton Van Schlemmer the Third, no less. A roaring pansy – but not at all of the *simpatico* type.'

Hope lowered her voice and inclined her head towards my mother's ear: '*Public lavatories*.' She gave an ironic laugh. 'I remember darling, *darling* Ursie saying to me: "I respect him, you see, because he reminds me of Father"! My dear, anything *less* like ...! But never mind. He claimed to come of good old Dutch stock and did have some money of his own but had lost it all trying to set up a Nigger Heaven which collapsed, I gather, through sheer inefficiency and sloppy management. Anyway, their engagement was announced, and then almost immediately something took place (I never quite knew what) which opened her eyes and she came to her senses and broke if off. My dear, *would* you believe it, the swine kicked up the most frightful song and dance and threatened to take her to court for breach of promise! That, at least, was the *official* version. But behind the scenes, what he was really up to was far, far worse – nothing short of blackmail! Unless you pay up, he said – or words to that effect – I intend to inform the Yellow Press that the first cousin once removed of a former British Ambassador to the United States of America is practising the Lesbian perversion with a noted actress as black as the ace of spades! Oh, it jolly nearly caused the most godal*mighty* scandal – it was touch and go! I can't tell you exactly what happened for the simple reason that I don't know – but I do know that Ursie's father was too wonderful and staunch and somehow or other strings were pulled and the situation was saved. But it *could* have been ugly. Very, very ugly indeed.'

As often with Hope's bombshells, there was something a little inconclusive and not entirely convincing about this one; in spite of the impression she produced of substantiating her story with graphic detail, I remained uncertain about what exactly had happened in it. My mother was also bemused.

'All that is fascinating,' she said, 'and yet it doesn't quite ring true to me. It's not that I'm surprised that Yvo didn't tell me about it. Apart from wanting to spare me anxiety, he had a horror of gossip and simply never repeated anything unpleasant about other people. I believe he had once confided something to my predecessor – Ursula's mother – and she passed it on to her sister, and a whole lot of mischief was made as a result. He always said one could never trust a woman with a secret – Shakespeare says the same thing somewhere, doesn't he? And I suppose he was right: I might easily have mentioned something about Ursula and this man, without thinking, to somebody else. But what I *can't* believe is that he would have been able to keep it from me if he had been seriously worried about her at that time. On the other hand, do you think it could have been that which brought on his illness? It was around then that he started having trouble with his heart ...'

'Would it have worried him?' I asked.

'Oh, unbearably – Ursula being unhappy, I mean, not the scandal, he wouldn't have minded that at all. He refused to admit that homosexuality even existed, you know: if I ever said that a friend of mine was queer, he would tease me about having a nasty mind. He would just have thought that his daughter was being persecuted by some motivelessly malevolent fiend, like Iago, and he would have suffered deeply for her sake. Poor angel, his loyalty to his loved ones did sometimes lead him to back the wrong horse – not in this case, of course, but I was thinking of a *cause célèbre* during the First War, before I entered the family. Do you remember it, Hope? Mrs Warburton-Wells.'

'Do I!' said Hope. 'I could pass an examination on it.'

Mrs Warburton-Wells was in fact the elder sister of my father's first wife – the one who had received, and betrayed, the fatal confidence. A 'professional beauty' and favourite of King Edward VII, she was famous for her boisterous high spirits and daring practical jokes. When she descended a staircase it was never on foot, but either sliding down the banisters or seated on a tray; once, when leaving Sandringham after a shooting party, instead of leaning out of the carriage and waving a last goodbye with her graceful arm, she had stuck an equally graceful leg out of the window and waved that.

'The Warburton-Wells affair was extremely unsavoury but wildly enjoyable,' said Hope. 'She was getting rather long in the tooth but still had plenty of pep so when the war broke out she turned her house into a convalescent home for wounded soldiers, both officers and men. She designed a most becoming uniform for herself and took some phoney title – Matron-in-Chief or Hospital Commandant or something – but really all she did was carry on with the patients. OK, bully for her, you might say – except that one of them wasn't having any, a young private who had just got engaged to be married. She was so livid with rage when he turned her down that she cooked up some story and tried to have the wretched boy court-martialled for cowardice, if you please! All the top brass were her ex-lovers so they backed her up to the hilt. If he'd been found guilty he'd have been shot at dawn – for not going to bed with Mrs Warburton-Wells! A bit much, don't you agree? But he managed to bring an action for slander against her first, which thank God he won, so justice was done in the end.'

'Well,' said my mother, 'all I know is that darling Yvo went willingly into the witness box to give evidence for her *defence*. He just could not believe that his own sister-in-law would be such a monster as to ruin the poor soldier merely because her sexual vanity had been hurt. As a rule he was absolutely right about everything – it was a mixture of sweet natural innocence and blind family loyalty that made him lose his judgment on this occasion.'

'There's a lot of him in Ursula,' said Hope.

After this, Hope's business trips to London ceased, and we felt ourselves further removed from Ursula than ever. My mother did, however, receive a letter from Ruby, giving a different Brooklyn address. 'Above, our new abode, where we have been in residence for the past month,' she wrote. 'Another letter was started, in which I told of my unhappiness at having to give up our very nice house and my complete dissatisfaction with this cramped, inconvenient and unsightly apartment – Ursula's valiant battle with the City Fathers having ended in defeat. But it did not seem fair to pass on to you my personal misery, so I destroyed it. And now, though in less detail and fewer words, I have managed to duplicate my original imposition. Forgive me! Ursula has planned a letter to you for some time, but she is quite worn out when she gets home in the evenings and her weekends are spent in recuperation. This from me is merely a "push" in the right direction ...' There was a terse postscript from Ursula: 'Be a saint and give the new address to all my friends. Have misplaced my address book in the move. No doubt will find it in a few years' time.'

But, in the end, Hope's prophecy that Ursula would never return to England proved to be false. Early in 1959, Ursula wrote to my mother that, in celebration of her recent retirement from the Veterans' Bureau with a pension and a 'handshake', she had decided to come over for three weeks in the spring – this time accompanied by Ruby, who was said to be eagerly looking forward to making the acquaintance of Ursula's family at last.

I had just started working on a glossy magazine, which paid slightly more than the publishing job had done, and we could now afford to dispense with the South American lodgers – so there was enough room in our house to accommodate Ursula and Ruby during their visit. My mother proposed giving a cocktail party in their honour, and asked them to send a list of the guests they wished her to invite. This reached us only ten days before they were due to arrive themselves; my mother happened to be abroad at the time, and so I had the task of ascertaining the whereabouts, if any, of their friends on the list (some of them once-celebrated names that had dropped out of common currency over the past thirty years) and running them to earth.

It was easy enough to trace Fleur. Having married, comparatively late in life and with a certain amount of publicity, she was now called Lady Carter-Banks and was listed under that name in the London telephone directory. But no sooner had I made this discovery, than another letter arrived from Ursula: Fleur, after all, was on no account to be invited because Ruby did not care to meet her and, should there be the slightest danger of Lady Carter-Banks appearing at the party, Ruby herself would refuse to attend it. 'Sorry if this has landed you in the soup,' Ursula wrote. 'If you'd be an angel and wire me Fleur's address I'll write to her and try to explain. I'll promise to come and see her on my own while I'm over there – I *think* Ruby can be persuaded to agree to that (*touch wood!*)'

Finding Bunch also presented no difficulty: she was even more famous than Fleur and, like her, had acquired a title, being now known as Dame Beryl Bunbury. She ran (among other concerns) a chain of shops selling cheap, chic fashion accessories which were successfully exported all over the world, and she had been awarded the DBE in recognition of her services to the national economy. When I rang her up she was extremely friendly – 'What *glorious* news!' – and she solved my remaining problems in tracking down the other people on the guest list, promptly providing the present addresses of such legendary black entertainers as Turner Layton and Elisabeth Welch.

'How thrilling,' I said. 'I used to love their records. Tell me, am I right in thinking that Ruby was never a singer herself?'

'Quite right. She can't sing a note.'

I explained that my insatiable curiosity about Ruby had led me to search for references to her in every possible source, and one of the few I had managed to find (in some obscure theatrical memoir of the 1920s) had described her singing a negro spiritual at a musical *soirée*. This had been puzzling me for ages.

'Oh, that wasn't her,' said Bunch. 'That would have been the other Ruby Richards.'

'The *other* Ruby Richards?'

'Yes. Wasn't it awful? There was another woman with exactly the same name – also black, and also on the stage. Ruby minded dreadfully about it: it couldn't have been more maddening. Both of them absolutely refused to change their names, so it all went on being frightfully confusing. You're not the first person to fall into that trap, by a long chalk. Anyone else I can help you with for the party?'

'What about Enid ffrench?'

'Oh dear, *too* sad – she died last year.'

'And Fay Hitchcock?'

Bunch hesitated before replying, and then chuckled. 'No, love, I'm afraid la Hitchcock *won't* be able to make it. It's all a bit embarrassing, but the truth is that she's landed herself in jug and is likely to stay there for quite some time.'

'Whatever for?'

'Assault. If she'd been a chap they'd have called it Grievous Bodily Harm.'

It seemed that Fay, after recovering from 'that whopping great nervous breakdown she had not long after the war', had found employment as a Gym and Geography mistress in an expensive boarding school for girls; unfortunately, during an argument with one of her favourite pupils, she had lost her temper to the point of punching the child on the jaw. There had been a muted scandal (reminiscent of *The Children's Hour*, the banned play that Fay had wanted to see twenty years ago) as a result of which the school had been forced to close down.

5

I had been speculating about Ruby with so obsessive an intensity for so many years – at least a quarter of a century – that I was prepared for our first meeting to contain an element of unreality; when I was finally confronted by her visible presence, it failed to make any impression on me at all. I had come home early from the office, to find her sitting at the dining-room table having tea with Ursula and my mother; I joined them, but after spending several hours in her company I would have been incapable of describing her appearance beyond the vaguest outline. However, I can fill in this dazzled blank and reconstruct what I must have seen from evidence provided by two photographs which I still possess.

One, taken on board the *Queen Elizabeth* during the voyage that had brought them over, shows four elderly ladies grouped cheerfully round a table in a room like a hotel lounge. At a first glance, they might be taken for Daughters of the American Revolution out on a decorous spree. Two of them – plump, matronly figures – appear to be sisters; a third, sitting bolt upright, slightly scowling and stiffly brandishing a cigarette, is Ursula – frozen by camera-shyness into an unnaturally formal pose. The fourth is a delicate little thing, with shining smooth silver hair and a radiant smile, elegantly clothed in a simple but expensive-looking black dress, clearly the star of the occasion: Ruby, who was then approaching her middle seventies. On the back of the picture, in Ruby's handwriting, are the words: The night I won 30 dollars at Bingo.

The second photograph was taken, without their knowledge, after they had landed. Ruby and Ursula are queuing at a desk before going through Immigration and Customs. Both are in profile. Concealed impatience has made Ursula's serious expression almost grim; her short hair has been pushed behind her ears and a wispy bit of veiling has been crookedly tied round her pudding-basin hat. Clearly tired, she stands in a slumped position with her elbow on the desk. Behind her, Ruby's head is uplifted to give her a mildly martyred look. Her smart tweed coat contrasts with Ursula's shabby fur; she wears a beret set far back over her silky *coiffure* and a spotted veil covers the upper part of her face, enhancing the attraction of her raised eyebrows, tiny tilted nose and shapely pouting mouth.

At tea, on that first day of their visit, Ursula looked much happier than she did in the photographs. 'I can't believe that we're all four actually together at last, sitting here in this sweet little house!' she said. 'I'm longing to explore the neighbourhood, which of course is full of memories for me. Ruby, I'm afraid you're in for a conducted tour! How well I remember, on Sunday mornings, playing tennis with Father in

Cadogan Square, then strolling up Sloane Street very pleased with myself for having taken all that exercise to meet my friends for lunch at the Hyde Park Hotel, which was a favourite haunt of ours. The barman there was famous for mixing the best White Lady in London.'

As part of my duties on the glossy magazine was to review plays, I had been given two seats for a matinée of *Othello* at Stratford-upon-Avon, starring Paul Robeson. I asked Ruby if she would like to come with me, as I knew Robeson was an old friend of hers. Ursula looked at her expectantly, her eyes bright with pleasure. Ruby accepted formally and gravely, but did not immediately appear to be overjoyed by the invitation. Some ten minutes later, however, when the conversation had passed on to other subjects, she slowly and deliberately cut off a sliver of cake from a larger piece that she had been about to eat. Balancing the morsel on her knife, she solemnly transferred it from her plate to mine. I looked at it in perplexity. 'That', she explained archly, 'is for *you*. To thank you for taking me to see Paul on Saturday.' She gazed at me fixedly for a while, and then turned to Ursula, who was anxiously watching this little drama. 'He's my buddy,' she said.

It was hoped that the Stratford outing would consolidate this promising *rapport* between Ruby and myself, and establish an even closer relationship. To some extent it did so. I had hired a chauffeur-driven car for the day and booked a table for lunch at a highly recommended hotel: this was to be an occasion. As it ceremoniously unfolded, two separate aspects of Ruby's personality were revealed to me. One was a frail, unassuming old lady, easily tired and anxious to please. The other was a self-conscious siren, who set a high price on the value of her company and (once this was understood) took pains to elevate any shared experience into the special category of a treat. Like the hero of a romantic American film, I seemed to be forever clutching the back of her chair as she serenely lowered herself into it; leaving the car by one door, rushing round behind it and opening the other to facilitate her exit; helping her in and out of her coat, holding her handbag and lighting her cigarette. It was as if the slight hint of a Southern drawl in her voice had confused me into attempting a slapdash caricature of old-world ante-bellum courtesy. Ruby kindly ignored the farcical element in this behaviour, and rewarded me by dignifying our adventure with an atmosphere of complicity, heightening the simple pleasures it afforded by subtly suggesting that we were a couple of kids playing hooky from authority – a gang of two.

We talked mainly about plays, films and books, but during lunch Ruby volunteered a few details of her family history. Her grandmother had been a slave on a Mississippi estate. At the age of fifteen she had been raped by a white man, the plantation owner's son. She died giving birth to his daughter. This child was smuggled to the North during the Civil War, grew up to be a beauty, and went on the stage. She married a gifted musician, who came from a prominent middle-class Negro family with lawyers, doctors and teachers among its members. They had eight children, one of whom was Ruby.

We just had time to peep at Anne Hathaway's cottage and Shakespeare's birthplace before the matinée began. Ruby was most complimentary about the design of the Memorial Theatre, declaring that it was far superior to any she had seen in the States. She also praised the production–'A *much* higher standard than you could find back home.' For me, both of these were of interest only as a background to Paul Robeson's performance, which had been disliked by most of the critics but which I found overwhelming. Some of the most beautiful lines ever written were spoken by one of the most beautiful voices ever heard. His impressive stature and physical strength made the gradual exposure of Othello's weakness seem to threaten an unthinkable cosmic disorder; when he crashed to the ground in a sudden fit, one recognised a primitive dread of some arbitrary last collapse; when he said: 'Chaos is come again', the rumble of the syllables sounded like a warning echo of the primordial void.

After the play, Ruby took me backstage to congratulate the star. We found him still standing in the wings, quite alone and at some distance from anybody else, naked to the waist, pouring with sweat and rubbing himself down with a towel–more like an athlete than a leading man. We approached him timidly. When he saw Ruby, he gave a roar of surprise and delight. I remained a few paces apart, to observe a long, intimate and animated conversation between the handsome giant and the fragile, dainty woman. The scene moved and deeply satisfied me, because it realised almost exactly one of the fantasies I had entertained so persistently since childhood about the exciting and exalted world which Ursula had entered when she went off to live with Ruby.

At a quarter to six on the day of the party, Ursula, Ruby, my mother and I were posted about the drawing-room in attitudes made artificial by apprehension: even the room looked quite unlike its usual self although no palpable alteration had been made to it. We could hear the ominous movements of the butler hired from Searcey's as he polished glasses and positioned bottles at a bar he had created in the dining-room across the narrow hall. Ursula was handsomely arrayed in a green and gold caftan; Ruby wore a pretty little cocktail dress which showed off her still beautiful breasts and legs. The knowledge that Ursula was longing for a drink, and that she had promised Ruby not to have one, raised the nervous tension of the waiting period beyond the norm: it was a long three quarters of an hour before the doorbell rang. But from that moment on, there were no more worries. Everybody on the original list turned up (except for Fay, Enid and Fleur), all eager to welcome the guests of honour, to tell them (and be told in return) how little they had changed after so long an absence and how deeply they had been missed.

It was Bunch more than anyone who made the party go. An air of authority, which I had sensed in her at our first meeting in the Wigmore Street flat when there had been little apparent justification for it, had matured and mellowed with her worldly success and now infused her rather gruff manner with a potent charm. She was extremely excited by the *Nouvelle Vague* and told us all about the brilliant young film directors in France, introducing into the occasion a heady feeling of being behind the scenes and in the know at the very latest thing, and thus saving it from too strong a dependence on nostalgic reminiscence. But she was equally adroit at evoking a pleasant past. 'Darling!' she called across to Ursula. 'Remember Punkadillo?'

Ursula was delighted. 'Can I ever forget him?'

'When I first knew Ursula, back in the 'twenties,' Bunch explained, 'she had this pet jerboa. A tiny little thing with enormous eyes, which moved in huge leaps like a kangaroo. I shall never forget the sensation she caused when she took it with her to tea at the Ritz.'

'Oh, no, I'm sure I never did that,' said Ursula. 'But I did once smuggle him into the cinema with me. I thought nobody had noticed – but a few days later I read in the paper that the movie-house was going to close as someone had reported seeing a rat in it! Fancy you remembering Punkie!'

Bunch took me aside and lowered her voice. 'Tell me, dear, before I put my foot in it – is Spencer still in the picture, do you happen to know?'

'No, I believe he died a few years ago.'

'Oh dear, poor soul. I wasn't certain whether to ask for news of him or not: the last I heard, he had become rather a trial.'

'Did you know him?'

'Yes, a bit, in the old days. He was awfully sweet, but *the* most tremendous lecher. I remember getting a terrible ticking off from Ursula because I wouldn't go to bed with him. She was simply livid. Accused me of every kind of racial prejudice, which I *did* think a little unfair ...' Seeing that Ruby was approaching us, she turned towards her and continued smoothly: 'I was just boasting about how long you and I have been friends. Bet you don't remember where and when we first met! It was at a party for the cast of *Four Saints in Three Acts* in New York in 1934! Freddie Ashton had invited me, and you and Ursula came with Carl Van Vechten.'

'And to this day', said Ruby, 'I can hear Ursula's cry of rapture when she saw you there. "*Bunch*!" She was in the seventh heaven.'

'But rather cross with me for being in New York without letting her know. I'd planned to surprise her, you see.'

'They did a revival of *Four Saints* a few years ago ...' Ruby began.

'I caught it when it came to Paris! Leontyne Price sang too divinely for any words. I can't tell you how moving it was to see Alice B. Toklas sitting in the audience ... so proud of Gertrude, and missing her so terribly.'

'I know, I know ... Carl keeps in close touch with Alice and sometimes reads us her letters. She sounds a perfect honey. She always calls Carl her Papa Woojums and he calls her his Mama Woojums – and Miss Stein of course was their Baby Woojums! I think that's so cunning, don't you?'

'Too sweet,' said Bunch rather drily. 'I must say, this *is* a joyful reunion – a real gathering of the clans, *non*? Now let's have a proper look and see who's here.' She dipped into one of the big, bold handbags that had become her trademark (and were sometimes just referred to as 'Beryl Bunbury bags'), extracted a glittering pair of harlequin spectacles, pushed them on to her nose and surveyed the room. '*So* many old chums ... I can't get over it. But I see no sign of Flash – or Fleur – or whatever she calls herself now. Couldn't she come?'

'If you are referring', said Ruby with saccharine sarcasm, 'to *Lady* Carter-Banks, I regret to say that Her *Lady*ship has been informed that her presence here would not be welcomed. And now, dear hearts, if you will excuse me, I see that a very special friend of mine has just arrived and is looking rather lost ...' She drifted off.

'Ouch!' said Bunch, making a rueful grimace. 'I seem to have put my big foot in it after all. The *way* she emphasised that title! Have you ever heard anything so sinister?'

'Do you know why she hates Fleur so much?'

'A bit of the green-eyed monster, but there's more to it than that. I believe it dates back to the very first time Ursula and Ruby met. Flash was there too, and perhaps she felt her nose had been put out of joint or something, anyway I understand that she said something tactless and patronising about black people, you know what a silly ass she can be when she gets on her high horse. I assumed it had been made up long ago, but apparently not.'

As often with successful parties, the festivity ended as abruptly as it began. Suddenly at nine o'clock there seemed to be a panic rush for the exit, leaving the room empty except for Ursula, Ruby, my mother, myself and Bunch, who announced that she was taking us all out to dinner at the Brompton Grill. It was a gently convivial meal, until Bunch made the innocent mistake of asking Ruby's opinion of Marlon Brando. 'I think he's such a marvellous actor. Weren't you in a play with him once, before he became famous? Do tell us what he's like.'

Ruby smiled fondly. 'Ah . . . my Marlon. How I love that boy! He has had the worst possible press, but in fact he is the kindest, most sensitive human being you could hope to find. He is just too good to be true – and vice versa. It seems impossible for him to avoid – how shall I phrase it? – female complications, put it that way. But none of us is perfect.'

Ursula looked stern. 'I hardly know him, but what I do know I can't say I care for. A very conceited young man indeed.'

Ruby continued: 'It so happened that, some years after I first met Marlon, I had to undergo a brief period of hospitalisation. In the intervening time, he had become a great star – but that did not prevent him from coming to visit me in the public ward. No, sirree! And you should have seen those young nurses when this celebrated Adonis came marching in – they were all swooning away like bobby-soxers! Oh, I got *very* special treatment after that, believe you me!'

'Why on earth shouldn't he come and see you?' said Ursula pugnaciously. 'I should hope he would. And I think it's shocking that the nursing staff made a pet of you as a result. When I was a VAD favouritism was strictly forbidden, and quite right too. What about all the other poor patients who didn't have the luck to know Marlon Brando?'

Ruby pretended not to hear. 'Oh, he's such a darling person! As you know, he is . . . what shall I say . . . extremely easy on the eye – and in the acting department he is a very, very great artist indeed. But also – and here I *do* know what I'm talking about – he is the loveliest and loyalest of friends.'

'Ruby's quite potty on this subject,' Ursula muttered. 'I wish she'd get off it.'

'And on top of all of that,' Ruby pursued, 'he is an extremely amusing companion. I remember, when he first became a buddy of mine, he had just been on tour in some vehicle for Tallulah which closed on the road . . .'

'I *hate* this story,' said Ursula, quite loudly. Ruby slightly turned her head and shoulders away from her, to concentrate on Bunch. 'And he was so comical about it!' she went on. 'It seems that in the old days Miss Bankhead had always taken it for granted that the juvenile lead would . . .'

'I refuse to listen to this!' Ursula interrupted, putting her hands over her ears.

'As you choose, my precious . . . the juvenile lead would – er – enter into a romantic relationship with her. It was kind of an old theatrical tradition, you see. But I'm afraid she was barking up the wrong tree with my Marlon! Oh my, oh my! His imitation of Miss B. trying to seduce him had us all in a roar! If only you'd heard him, Bunch, you'd have died laughing. I'm not the brilliant mimic he is so I can't do justice to her husky voice and deep,

deep Southern accent, but apparently one night she ...'

'Stop it!' Ursula shouted. 'If you go on with this dirty libel on Tallulah, I warn you, I shall go straight home! All right, so maybe she *did* make a pass at him, but what's so hysterically funny about that? He should have thought himself damned lucky, in my opinion. You seem to forget that Tallulah is an old and dear friend of mine and, whatever her faults, she is in her own way a very fine and brave and beautiful person. I can't *stand* hearing her talked about in this degrading way – and what is more I *won't* stand it! And don't try to make out I'm tipsy, because I stayed on the wagon all day!'

Ruby leaned forward and clasped Ursula's hand. 'I *know* you did, darling heart, and all honour to you! Of *course* I won't continue with the anecdote if it upsets you. This has been such a heavenly evening, it would be a wicked shame to spoil it now. So – a ban on Marlon and Tallulah from now on!' She earnestly pressed Ursula's hand and slowly withdrew her own. Then, turning to Bunch, she added in an undertone: 'I'll tell you the rest some other time, if it interests you. It was silly of me to forget how *crazily* jealous she always becomes at the mere mention of that boy.'

Ursula, fortunately, did not hear this. With glistening eyes, she was herself whispering to me: 'I'm so sorry to make a scene. People say it clears the air but I'm afraid it does the reverse. I just couldn't help it, though. I'm positive she was trying to provoke me on purpose, and the only reason I can think of is that she wanted to punish me for going to see poor old Flash while *she* was off gallivanting with you at the theatre.'

6

A year after their return to America we heard that Ursula and Ruby had moved house once again. Their new apartment – still in Brooklyn – was in a large tower block. It was small, but skilfully designed for maximum comfort and equipped with every possible labour-saving device. They loved it. We could glimpse a corner of it in a coloured photograph they sent us, which showed them both, happily smiling, sitting side by side on a sofa. They were wearing the clothes they had worn at my mother's cocktail party; a portrait in oils of my father as a young subaltern in the 16th Lancers, painted in the 1880s, hung on the wall behind them. On the back was written: 'Christmas, 1960. Ain't she beautiful? Love Ursula' and beneath that: 'Ain't *she* beautiful! Love Ruby'.

There followed a presumably contented silence of four years, and then suddenly I received a letter from Ruby. 'I have taken the liberty', she wrote, 'of giving your name and address to a friend of mine who will be in London shortly, and of asking him to present my greetings to you. I did so because I am sure it would be a mutually agreeable acquaintance. I mentioned the possibility of your being out of the city so he is quite prepared to miss you. However I will appreciate the courtesy of your permitting him to call on you, if it will be convenient. He is about your age, a charming person who shares with you an interest in things theatrical. He was assistant stage manager on *Twenty-Eight Young Men Bathe by the Shore*, a fact that we small fry in the company resented because, knowing him to be a very rich young man, we felt that someone less affluent should have the job. *Young Men* was not far into its phenomenal success before we learned to love him. He is now producing on his own, mainly in the off-Broadway field, and I daresay his visit to London has something to do with theatre. Naturally he will be busy for he is certainly not a dilettante and may not have the leisure to contact you. But if he does you will know who he is and why I want you two to know each other. I hope all is well with you very dear folks, who have a place in my heart and in my prayers. Fondly, Ruby. P.S. I nearly forgot! *Beau Maclean* is the name of the gentleman in question.'

Beau Maclean must have been as busy during his London trip as Ruby predicted – or possibly it was cancelled at the last moment; at all events, I heard nothing from him. But any disappointment that this minor anti-climax might have caused me was soon overwhelmed by excitement in the knowledge that, after waiting so long, I was actually on the point of going to America myself. I had recently left the glossy magazine for a job on the colour supplement of a Sunday newspaper, and one of my first foreign assignments, early in 1965, was to interview a famous actress who was filming on location in Mexico. I would have to fly out direct to Mexico City, but on the way back I could arrange to break the journey for a night or two in New York.

So my first experience of that city came after a bewildering fortnight spent in the hysterical atmosphere of big-budget multinational movie-making, where journalists were simultaneously courted and kept at bay, against the inhospitable background of the fierce Mexican landscape; by contrast New York, with its cosy skyscrapers and friendly freeways, seemed reassuringly familiar. As the plane touched down, I had a sense of return rather than arrival; riding in a yellow cab from the airport to the Gramercy Park Hotel, I felt the placid anticipation of a traveller who is nearing home. By the time I had checked in and unpacked, it was early evening: I rang Ursula and Ruby (it was the latter who answered) to tell them I was on my way.

But things did not at first go smoothly. On the previous night a taxi driver had been murdered in Brooklyn and now I found that driver after driver refused to take me there. Realising that I was going to be late, I started to panic. At last one man, albeit repressively, allowed me to enter his cab. I had written the address on a piece of paper, which I gave him. He glanced at it, then told me that he had no idea where it was but would put me down somewhere in the neighbourhood. Unlike the New York cabbies in Hollywood films, who incessantly and wittily converse over their shoulders with their fares, this one didn't speak a word throughout the journey. As we crossed the Brooklyn Bridge (which did look as hallucinatory as it does in films) I fancied that the back of his head might have belonged to Charon, silently ferrying an apprehensive passenger over the Styx.

He stopped the car, apparently in obedience to some arbitrary decision, after about half an hour's drive on the Brooklyn side, speechlessly accepted the money I gave him, then shot off. Conscious of having been dumped, I stood on the kerb, at a loss. My surroundings appeared to be entirely without character; I might have been in any town in any country; there seemed to be no passers-by. Brooklyn, I knew, was immense: would I ever find my way? I walked on a few paces, until I came to a crossroads, where instinct made me turn to the left. I was looking down another long, equally featureless street, at the far end of which a solitary female figure could be seen in the dusk, standing erect and peering in every direction like an anxious sentry, clearly on the lookout for an awaited stranger. The figure waved: it was Ursula. As impervious to surprise as a dreamer, I walked to meet her with the complacent lack of haste that follows a reprieve.

Relief at my arrival increased her natural reserve and she was almost as taciturn as the taxi driver while she hurried me into the building. We emerged from the elevator on the eighteenth floor and walked down a corridor towards the distant figure of Ruby framed in the open door of their apartment, her arms extended in greeting. 'Welcome, welcome!' she cried, as soon as we came within earshot. When I got nearer, I saw that she was holding a glass containing whisky, soda and ice already mixed. She presented this to me before we embraced. 'I did not want you to have to wait *one extra second* before tasting your very first drink in our Home Sweet Home!'

She led me through a minute hallway into a small, bright, crowded room, filled with plants and cut flowers. The furniture was new and plain while the pictures and ornaments were antique and elaborate. Ruby settled me into a comfortable armchair. 'Now you just relax and enjoy a cosy chat with your beloved sister while I fix something for our supper. She's been so blissfully excited ever since she knew you were coming! And just this once, as a special treat to mark the occasion, she's going to have a highball too!'

Ruby ceremoniously handed Ursula a drink and then moved gracefully behind a waist-high partition which divided the kitchen from the living area. Ursula gazed after her, almost as if she had never seen her before, and murmured: 'She walks in beauty ...'

'What nonsense!' said Ruby. 'Don't forget, I'll be eighty next birthday!'

'You weren't supposed to hear,' said Ursula. Turning her attention to me, she saw that I was studying a painting on the wall. It was a portrait of my father's mother in old age. 'Isn't that lovely of darling Grumps? You never knew her, did you? What you missed! How you would have adored her! I've always said, I've been lucky enough in my life to know two saints. One was Grumps – and the other is over there in the kitchen at this moment, cooking her own very special chili con carne! Wait one moment and I'll show you something that will interest you ...' She fetched a volume from a low bookshelf in the hallway and placed it in my hands. 'My most treasured possession. Grumps's Bible.'

Bound in white vellum, the Bible had been transformed by my grandmother into a combination of personal diary, family history and commonplace-book. Flowers and grasses had been pressed between its pages and also tiny loose photographs, faded to the same pale brown; favourite passages had been underlined, or copied out in the margins and on the flyleaves; the births, marriages and deaths of children, grandchildren and even some great-grandchildren had been recorded in her ample Victorian hand – and between the years 1914 and 1918 the deaths in battle of more distant relations and of the sons of friends had been added to the Roll of Honour. Beside a drawing of two attenuated angels in the manner of Burne-Jones she had written: 'The more of those whom we love that God takes unto Himself, the greater the Communion of Saints with all our Beloveds. Easter Sunday, April 20th, 1919'. One photograph larger than the others had been pasted on to the inside of the back cover. This showed Ursula, wearing school uniform and a straw boater, seated on a bench in a town square between her grandparents, a distinguished white-haired couple dressed in formal black, while a greyhound and a dachshund, vague as apparitions formed by ectoplasm, wandered out of focus away from the camera's scrutiny. Beneath it were the words 'June 1910 – the day we went to London – our last season – sweet of darling Ursie but Fly and Welcome refused to sit still!!!' On the opposite page two quotations had been transcribed, one from the Old Testament and one from the New: 'He that covereth a transgression seeketh love; but he that repeateth a matter separateth very friends (Proverbs, 17:9)' and 'Love worketh no ill to his neighbour; therefore love is the fulfilling of the law (Romans, 13:10)'.

'Come and get it!' Ruby called out gaily, untying the apron she had put on to protect her elegant white trouser suit. We joined her at a card-table covered by a lace cloth on which three places had been invitingly laid.

Before starting the meal Ruby paused for a while in a significant manner, as if about to say grace. 'I just want you to know', she said at last, 'how proud I am to offer hospitality to a member of my darling's family. I don't think anything could truly mar the happiness of the years we have spent together – but I confess that I have had my one little private cause for sadness. And that is the nagging sense of guilt that – through my fault, however unwittingly – she has been separated for so long from her own flesh and blood and the land of her first allegiance. Your presence here this evening eases that feeling of – no, not remorse, let us say of *regret* – just a little bit.'

I was wondering what on earth to reply to this when Ursula came to my rescue. 'Don't, darling, please,' she said to Ruby. 'We've *been* through this so often before. I knew exactly what I was doing all along and there is nothing for anyone to regret. Well, I don't know about you guys, but I'm ravenous,' she went on cheerfully. 'Gosh, this looks good – do let's start. To tell you the truth,' she said to me while we ate, 'we're both a bit shaken by the death of Malcolm X. I expect you read about his assassination last week. The police are trying to make out that he was killed by the Black Muslims.'

'His own people,' said Ruby bitterly. 'In the bad old days, when an atrocity was committed against a member of my race, it was so easy to feel indignation against the whites. Now, it isn't so simple. I find that peculiarly distressing.'

'I *hate* extremism and violence as much as anyone,' said Ursula. 'Everything in me longs for moderation and peace. But when years and years of moderation and peaceful protest produce so little result, one can at least understand *why* you get a frightening fanatic like Elijah Muhammad.'

'Maybe,' said Ruby. 'But I also understand that such people do immeasurable – perhaps even fatal – harm to the cause that they claim to espouse.'

'Anyway, I'm by no means convinced that it happened the way they say it did,' said Ursula. 'I shouldn't be surprised if the FBI wasn't behind the whole thing.'

'Oh, let's not talk politics tonight – it's so boring for our guest,' said Ruby. Before I could remonstrate, she addressed me directly. 'We've planned a great treat for you after supper. You're going to meet a really lovely person, our very dearest friend in all the world. We're taking you to see Bobby Smith.'

'Not *the* Bobby Smith? The pianist?'

'Yes, *the* Bobby Smith!' said Ursula triumphantly. 'There – I told you he'd know all about him.'

'I only know that he ran a wonderful nightclub

called Bobby's Place which I used to read about and longed to visit,' I said.

'Very few English people have heard of him because he's never been out of the States,' said Ruby. 'But I'd say that throughout the 'thirties Bobby's Place was just about the most glamorous joint uptown. Everybody went there but it never got ruined. Bobby's taste, and the sheer charm of his personality, managed to keep it exclusive.'

'I think you're rather giving the wrong impression by calling it "exclusive",' said Ursula. 'I'm sure Bobby never wanted to keep anybody out.'

'Of course not – he's the most unsnobbish person that ever lived – but we must face the fact, darling, that the basic idea of any club is to limit its clientele to a certain type of member,' said Ruby. 'It was the people who patronised it, as much as the music and entertainment they went to enjoy, that gave it such a pleasant atmosphere.'

'Anyway, it's been closed now for about twenty-five years,' said Ursula. 'But he still lives in a beautiful apartment only a few doors away from where Ruby was living when I first came over here and where I myself spent so many happy and exciting years. I know you'll love Bobby: he's a pussy-cat. The car's on the blink, so I can't drive you – just as well, no doubt, as I intend to have another highball when I get to Bobby's. We'll have to take a cab.'

Luckily, taxi drivers did not seem nervous of *leaving* Brooklyn – not even to go to Harlem, where there had been recent riots in the wake of Malcolm X's murder. Sitting in a cab between

Ursula and Ruby, I crossed the magical bridge again; once on the other side, we all three became infected by the party spirit and started to sing Rodgers and Hart's 'Manhattan' in loud tuneless voices.

The party spirit accompanied us into Bobby's flat, where it rose to an almost Bacchanalian pitch. The place seemed purpose-built for revelry – fantastic as a pleasure-dome, ephemeral as a painted backcloth or circus tent. The walls were black, the curtains were gold, the furniture was upholstered in plum velvet, the bar was decorated by silver stars on a ground of midnight blue. The general effect was of a ballet design by Bakst crossed with the dream night-nursery of a precocious little girl.

Bobby, a black man in his sixties, looked as young and lean and supple as he had in his heyday when his nickname had been 'Snakehips Smith'. The powerful attraction which he exerted was generated by a combination of elegant refinement and affectionate spontaneity. After embracing us all and calling us 'Pussy-cat', he set out to show us a good time. He sat down at a white grand piano and played and sang: smart show tunes with saucy lyrics by Cole Porter, tragic love songs which had become identified with the mythic martyrdom of Billie Holiday, traditional spirituals which had been given a new resonance by Martin Luther King. He performed without appearing to seek applause but with the modest generosity of a host putting a new LP on the record player for the amusement of his guests. Then he entertained us with anecdotes about Bobby's Place in its palmy days and the fascinating people – gangsters, boxers, film stars, kings – who had come there.

'Hey – I've an idea,' said Ruby. 'Ursula hasn't seen her long-lost brother for ages and he's only in town for one night. They must have so much to talk over. So why don't Bobby and I go into the room next door and give them a little precious time alone together? Because we've got plenty to talk about as well, haven't we, Pussy-cat?'

As it happened, Ursula and I didn't have a lot to say to each other; but there was nothing awkward about the silence that soon fell between us. We were like two constant companions who have no need to converse, enjoying a night out at a favourite haunt – perhaps at Bobby's Place, which I could imagine having reopened its ghostly doors after a quarter of a century to provide a congenial setting for our quiet celebration. It seemed to me that I had at last learned the answer to a question I had been asking ever since, at the age of five, I had heard a band on a boat play 'I'm a Dreamer – Aren't We All?' and I felt a sense of calm fulfilment.

Ursula's face wore a contented expression although there were tears in her eyes. 'I'm so glad you've met Bobby,' she said after a while. 'His existence takes a great load off my mind. My one big worry for years and years has been who would take care of Ruby when I kicked the bucket. My pension dies with me, of course, and so does the tiny income I still get from what was left of our family fortune. I've saved and saved all my working life and I'm glad to say there's a nice little sum in escrow – absolutely and *sacredly* untouchable by me while I live – that she'll inherit. But the important thing is that, so long as Bobby is around, I know she'll be lovingly looked after and won't be lonely.'

After another comfortable silence, she began to talk about the past, before I was born. 'It was wonderful in a way, I suppose. And one was always surrounded by love. Yet I was never as happy as perhaps I should have been. It was all that goddam privilege that stuck in my throat. I don't mean that it was abused by my parents and grandparents – though, heaven knows, there were some perfectly ghastly specimens among their family and friends, callous and selfish and worldly people like – well, I'd better not name names. Your darling mother would know who I mean – though she's always been so sweet and has such vitality that she managed to get on with them all without minding too much. I'm afraid I wasn't very good at that. But even with the wonderful ones, like Grumps – well, I suppose I really felt that *nobody* could be *quite* wonderful enough to justify that amount of privilege. Because all privilege must be won at the expense of other people's deprivation. And what could justify that? When I told Ruby, at dinner, that I've never regretted anything, I meant it. But of course she is right in thinking that I have sometimes been terribly homesick. Not for the place (though I do still miss riding on the Wiltshire downs!) but for the people: for Grumps and Jack and . . .' A sob forced her to pause.

'We've never really spoken about . . .' (she couldn't say the word 'Father') 'have we? It's agony, how I miss him. When he died . . . I've felt so terrifyingly bereft ever since. And in a way before that, too. Did I make him suffer a very great deal? I never quite knew. He said not. The last time I saw him, he said . . . he told me that . . . that all he wanted . . .' She was now crying so much that she could not continue. She looked at me through her tears – in supplication, in panic, in trust, in torment – trying to tell me something.

I knew what it was, or thought I did. Something about the dreadful simplicity of true goodness, the infuriating innocence which can accept, and perhaps rightly dismiss as irrelevant, those minor vices (pathetic snobbery, insecure egotism, scared conventionality) which madden the more complicated and drive them to desperate measures. Something also about that legacy of absolute love which is intended to shield one through life like a magic cloak but instead leaves one indecently disarmed and vulnerable to the most trivial adversary. I sat with Ursula in this exotic room, surrounded by signed photographs of Mabel Mercer, Bricktop and Florence Mills, while she wept for the old Edwardian days at Stars – not because she wanted them back again, but because of her nightmarish suspicion that she had never really left them.

The tears stopped, but she went on helplessly looking at me. Then she said: 'I'm afraid I've allowed myself to get a little drunk. Ruby would want me to go home.' Both of us somewhat dishevelled, we stumbled hand in hand into the next room where Bobby and Ruby were waiting. Sleek, sophisticated and composed, they turned to greet us in loving sympathy.

7

Two and a half years later, just before her seventieth birthday, Ursula died of cancer of the bone. In reply to my letter of condolence, Ruby wrote: 'I could never make up to Ursula for all she has meant to me. Everywhere I turn or look–everything I touch–are reminders of what we shared and enjoyed together bringing back memories of her magnificent character. I only wish you could have known her during her years in this country when, though totally inexperienced and unprepared for the rat race, she carved out a comfortably successful career and was respected and admired by all who were fortunate enough to come into contact with her. One day I shall send you letters from her superiors in office to confirm this. When Mrs Roosevelt passed, Adlai Stevenson said of her: "She would rather light a candle than curse the darkness." The same is true of our darling and the glow from all the candles she has lit in her lifetime will never die.'

Ruby herself lived to be ninety. In her will, she left me Grumps's Bible.

The Ground Hostess

'Still when, to where thou wert, I came
Some lovely glorious nothing I did see.'
John Donne, 'Air and Angels'

The telephone rang. It had to be Hurricane Harriet.

'Hi,' she said.

'Hi. Listen, I can't talk now ...'

'You sound funny. Is something the matter? Look, why don't I come over right ...'

'No,' I said in a panic, and I hung up on her. The telephone rang again at once. This time it was Jeremy – who else? 'Hi,' he said.

'Hi. Sorry, but this isn't an awfully good moment ...'

'Oh, my dear, how awful. Are you all right? You sound a bit odd. If anything's the matter I could always whiz straight round ...'

'Nothing's the matter. I'll ring you later. 'Bye for now.' And I hung up on Jeremy too. But I still couldn't concentrate.

Something had to be done.

I always knew she'd die some day and I always

dreaded it and now it's happened. So what? So where does one go from here? Nowhere. Stay put. If they'd only let one. If they'd only ...

No, that isn't the right beginning. Start again. From scratch. But where's scratch? Ah, if one only knew *that* ...

For the first few weeks the letters of condolence flopped through the box in a steady spate. Variously combining conventional expressions of sympathy with licensed emotional indulgence, they gave a total effect of slightly smug hysteria. Some of them read like reasoned reviews – of a life, not a book or a play: all, naturally, 'raves'. It was almost an agony to open each one, and yet they *were* vaguely comforting, and comforting in their vagueness: at least they made some comment on my obsession, for although grief may sometimes imagine that it wishes its privacy respected, in fact it senses insult when it is ignored. Replying brought a tiny, masturbatory release; the least welcome were those with a well-meaning postscript: 'On no account, what*ever* you do, must you *dream* of answering this – you must be inundated!' Then the flood degenerated into a tardy trickle – startled, apologetic or impertinently reproachful: 'Why did nobody tell me sooner?' Some of these struck a subtly hectoring note: 'Please be *sure* to let me know if there is to be a memorial service!'

So there was one. The arrangements for this were supposed to 'take my mind off' by giving me something to do: they gave me something to do, but their essential irrelevance to the obsession only fixed it more securely in the forefront of my mind. When it was over, the trickle continued for a little while (with excuses for not having been able to attend and with congratulations – reviews again – on the success of the occasion) and then suddenly the whole thing stopped altogether. But the obsession, if anything, increased. The service, though religious in form, had been too social in spirit to work the intended trick of exorcism. A blank remained to be filled. Bereavement began.

A memoir. That might be the answer. Several of the letters, taking a cautious peep on the bright side, had suggested that *now*, with all the time in the world, I might be able at last to get down to some serious writing. A memoir of the mother I had lost. Of course it would be very difficult to do, perhaps even impossible, and nobody must know of my plan: secrecy would be an insurance against failure. But the harder my self-imposed task proved to be, the nearer it might come to filling that blank. Don't tell a soul. Just *do* it.

Soon, then, every evening after work at the office, my formerly reluctant steps from the Underground station to the empty flat would be impelled by a sense of purpose. As for the weekends, they would seem a luxurious orgy of stillness, like a cool clearing in the jungle towards which I had been hacking my way all week. The lonely evenings, the uncharted wastes of Saturday and Sunday, were to be filled by literary endeavour. The sadness of my solitude could thus itself be turned to advantage – for the activity of writing is known to be an essentially isolated struggle, and the necessary conditions for its practice are not available to all.

I had forgotten about my friends.

There is a form of loneliness so complete that it transcends any need for human companionship; it is an end in itself, a pure state of possibly fruitful suffering. This is not, however, readily acknowledged by outsiders. My friends were kind; they wanted to help; and help took the fairly regular form of ringing me up to suggest a meeting. I have always felt vulnerable when answering the telephone, as if I were naked; indeed, sometimes I *was* naked when it rang. Cravenly, I fell in with any sociable plan that was proffered. This made it difficult to get on with the memoir.

What am I saying? It made it *impossible* to *start* the memoir. And the recurring dream began – not a nightmare (it was quite pleasant) but none the less disturbing. In the dream she was still alive, still there: everything I remembered about the death had been the result of some sort of silly mistake. The grim cremation, the exalted memorial service, had been elementary errors, quite easy to explain away should anybody ask me about them. The notice in the 'deaths' column of the *Daily Telegraph* was potentially embarrassing – but nobody seemed to have seen it anyhow, so perhaps it didn't matter. In my dream I felt a mixture of slight anxiety that I could have made such a mysterious muddle and deep, calm, fulfilled relief. When I woke, I felt a mixture of mild assuagement that I hadn't, after all, made such a fool of myself and acute disillusionment followed by renewed sorrow.

I told my doctor that I couldn't sleep and he prescribed some pills which prevented me from dreaming, but I was still balanced enough to know that the Mogadons were a remedy rather than a cure and that only the finished memoir could reconcile me to my spiritually amputated condition and put an end to the period of mourning. What little time I managed to reserve for myself was wasted in embarking on aimless walks and making pointless lists (of Margaret Millar's novels, or Danielle Darrieux's films) although there were still things I couldn't do (play Lisa Della Casa singing *Beim Schlafengehen* on the gramophone) and places I couldn't visit (the house in St Luke's Road with a bronze plaque in memory of W. H. Hudson) because they either reminded me of her and therefore of death or of death and therefore of her. I kept on telling myself: 'I mustn't be rushed.' Somehow or other, the friends had to be warned off, kept at bay. I desired the hitherto unattainable – to be left alone: what Henry James once described as 'uncontested possession of the long, sweet, stupid day': that peace to which no living creature has a natural right.

Yes, for a time I was decidedly neurotic on the subject of my friends. I even imagined a kinship with Dorothy Edwards, who wrote two remarkable books in the late 1920s, was taken up by Bloomsbury and then killed herself, giving as her reason (or so I had been told) that she had too many friends and didn't like them. But soon I realised that most of my acquaintances had no wish to intrude on my precious privacy and were on the contrary only too happy to leave me to my own devices. The merest hint (that I was tentatively engaged on some unexplained 'work' and needed time to myself) was sufficient, as it turned out, to silence the telephone. I must admit to having felt a slight, illogical pang of resentment at finding myself so blandly abandoned, and the pang might have developed into a palpable hurt if the silence had been total. But it wasn't. Two of my friends – perhaps, as these things are reckoned, the two 'greatest' – refused to accept the new regime. Hints, in their case, were not enough; they demanded details and assumed that I would welcome their inhibiting desire for participation. Harriet was interested in herself and Jeremy was interested in me, both to the point of monomania: I don't know which was the more exhausting. For her, I was an audience – convulsed with laughter or purged by pity and terror; for him, I was the show itself. Such intense relationships are stimulating when life is going smoothly, but they can take a lot out of you if you aren't feeling quite up to the mark.

Harriet was involved in a protracted and painful divorce from her third husband, a rich man who had craftily gone to an aggressive young woman solicitor while Harriet was stuck with the stuffy old family firm, so that it looked as if she would emerge from the case with very little of his money. Her latest novel had just been published and was receiving patronisingly dismissive reviews; in it this husband was clearly identifiable as one of the less attractive characters. Meanwhile, she was herself bringing an action for libel against a journalist who had printed something disrespectful about her in a gossip column. One of her daughters was undergoing a cure for heroin addiction and her son had recently been sacked from Stowe just before sitting his A levels. She lived with a mild young man who was beginning mildly to bore her and she was blatantly on the lookout for a more exciting lover. She would come to me for advice with a solemn yet perfunctory insistence, as though consulting the I Ching, and would sometimes volunteer some disconcerting advice of her own. Small, blonde and assertive, she had the unsettling charm of a ferocious nature tempered by a cosy disposition.

Jeremy might be described as a professional fan. All his energies had been channelled into enthusiasms outside himself which he expressed in a manner bordering on the manic. In his moral make-up, the extrovert element had been overdeveloped like some hyperactive gland; his lack of ego was so spectacular that it paradoxically drew attention to itself. Self-deprecation ran riot in Jeremy, turned inside out and emerged as aggression; violent in his humility, he was a reverse image of that old Warner Brothers cliché, the sensitive gangster. He had read every recent book (often before it came out), seen every current opera, ballet, play or fringe revue; he was as exhaustive as the information columns in *Time Out* or *What's On* and his many friends, puzzled as to how he found time to cover so wide a field, sometimes caught themselves wondering whether he might not employ a team of researchers ... But there was nothing split, let alone multiple, about his personality; having cast himself as an ideal audience, he had the serene integrity of a collective noun. Tall, dark and very thin, he was insistently generous and relentlessly lively; his interest appeared never to wane. Both he and Harriet had a power to stimulate which made them irresistible; but they also shared (after lack of resistance in their interlocutors had assumed a pathological tinge) the power to deplete.

A typical evening: I entered the flat, put on my dressing-gown, poured myself a drink and opened a tin for the cat. These routine actions, briskly performed, were followed by an uncertain pause. What next? Perhaps there was something on the television. After a long wait a juddering green and mauve herring-bone pattern galvanised itself into an advertisement cartoon about a bouncing blob called Tommy the Thermostat ... I averted my gaze, which happened to fall on the writing-table. If at that moment I had caught sight of my bed I would probably have climbed into it instead, but as it was – why not sit at the table and work? It suddenly seemed possible. So I prised open the typewriter, twiddled in a stiff quarto sheet, and started. Not the memoir – not yet – but something less ambitious, a kind of warm-up, just to get back into the habit of thinking in words. This story, let's say: how did it begin? 'The telephone rang. It had to be Hurricane Harriet.' And then the telephone rang ...

'What's the *matter* with them all?' she demanded. 'Are they all demented, or what? Would somebody kindly explain to me, please? Because it's way beyond *me*. I give up ... The reviewers, I'm talking about, who else? Some of my very best work went into that book and they're treating it like a Mills & Boon potboiler, it just doesn't make sense. I don't expect them to give me the Nobel Prize, for Christ's sake – I do know my own limitations, only too well, alas! – but isn't it rather peculiar that not *one* of them so far has spotted the perfectly obvious point that the whole thing is meant to be an allegory of Good and Evil? I promise I'm not going potty or anything like that, but I do sometimes wonder whether there might not be some sort of conspiracy at work here. Doesn't it strike you as a *leetle* bit odd that they all seem to say exactly the same thing? As if they'd been primed: the word has gone out – get Harriet! And don't you think that it just conceivably might *not* be a coincidence that every single one of them is a MAN? Listen to this snide bastard in the *Listener*, and I quote: 'if the word "compassionate" did not already exist I'm afraid it would have to be invented to describe *Bleeding*. The authoress, who is clearly in love with her heroine, is so busy saying "yes" to life that she neglects to provide more than the barest minimum of characterisation, narrative structure or plot, unquote. Did you notice that "authoress"? Well, there's a giveaway, for a start. I mean, this is 1979 we're living in, right? No wonder this bigoted ignoramus can't understand that my emphasis on the theme of menstruation is merely a reworking of the Little Red Riding Hood myth in a post-modernist mode! What never ceases to amaze me is the way they all make the same stupid mistake and complain that I haven't written a totally different novel to the one that I set out to write. Why just one of them can't quite simply sit down and review the book in front of him, which has been sent to him for that purpose and for which no doubt he is getting handsomely paid ... oh, who cares anyway? To hell with the lot of them. Hasten, Jason, bring the basin – they make me *sick*!'

And there she left me, *planté* by the telephone, gazing across at the writing-table a few feet away, but now so incapacitated by the strain of trying to match her mood of indignation that to cross this space had become a physical impossibility. Closing my eyes, I made a concentrated effort to banish Harriet's words from my mind ... and as this began to succeed I comforted myself with the notion that perhaps her interruption had not after all been entirely negative in its effect. The story was clearly a mistake, not so much a rehearsal for the memoir as an alternative to confronting the challenge it presented. A memoir (surely this hardly needed to be said?) involved a conscious and sustained act of remembering, but my injured sensibilities were still instinctively united in a defensive flight away from grief towards forgetting. Instead of shrinking from memory, I must plunge into its depths: the shock of total recall might be brutal enough to numb the pain that would inevitably follow. It was dread of this pain which had brought about, as an inconvenient side effect, the mental paralysis from which I was suffering. I started to steer my thoughts, gingerly at first, in the desired direction, and was feeling that some progress might have been made when the telephone rang once more.

'You mustn't be cross,' Jeremy announced, 'but

I've done something which I really believe may help to bust your writer's block! No, listen a moment, don't say anything now – I warn you I'm going to be very Aries about this and you may not like it but I don't care! There's somebody I admire *enormously* – I'm not going to tell you his name just yet, but you must take my word for it that he's simply *brilliant*. Sensitive and subtle and tremendously point-seeing and really one of *us* – a very rare and remarkable and special person, actually. He's a publisher, but not a ghastly one at all. I know it sounds poncey and I do loathe the word, but the only way to describe his quality is to say that he's an *artist*. Well, I've told him about you ... What do you mean, *what* about you? Naturally I've told him that it's a tremendous secret but that you're working on something at the moment which *I happen to know* is going to be extremely remarkable and quite extraordinary and he'd be crazy if he didn't sign you up at once with an enormous advance. I also suggested that he ought to be rather firm with you about a deadline, because he's such a civilised creature – so unlike you-know-who, the *dreaded* – that he might have wanted not to seem too beady and tough and the whole thing might fizzle out which I think would be a *tragedy*. I won't say any more. Forget about the whole thing if you can't face it. I'd love to go on talking for hours but, alas, I've got to fly ... I'm meeting someone at the NFT – the William Wellman retrospective – it's terribly late and *I've* got the tickets ...'

Such interruptions as these continued to be a daily occurrence throughout a period of several weeks, during which I was indeed able to think about the memoir at regular intervals but only as a finished object, while remaining quite incapable of guessing at its possible contents. My reveries were taken up with visualising the dust jacket, seeking a title with the correct amount of characters in it to balance my name in harmonious typographical proportion, toying with the ideas of an allusive dedication (but to whom?) or an introductory quotation from my favourite poem by John Donne, rehearsing the terms of restrained self-promotion in which to couch the perfect blurb. I was relieved to find that reflections of this nature still achieved a satisfactory standard of consecutive coherence as far as they went, but depressed to discover that they always stopped short of any concrete anecdote, telling phrase or evocative incident which might have formed the basis for an opening paragraph of the actual text. When it reached that point, my mind seemed automatically to shift from one gear to another – or, rather, to stick in some vague and motionless condition in between. However, there was one occasion when it seemed that the vital transition might be made – when, like a curly cloud glimpsed in the far distance of a parched desert landscape, an episode came back to me out of the past that seemed to offer itself as a candidate for re-creation, even already accompanied by a few words that might serve as a start in the delicate task of describing it ... but the words were scattered and the memory shrivelled at the sound of the telephone bell.

Harriet began the conversation with a statement: 'I'm interrupting your dinner.' Her tone was intended to suggest contrition but the words none the less emerged as an accusation. 'No, of course you're not,' I stuttered in self-defence. 'That's all right then,' she said. 'It's just that you sounded as if you had your mouth full ... Well, I've written a thriller and I may be quite mad but of course I think it's really rather brilliant. You've just *got* to read it as soon as possible and tell me *exactly* what you think. Be as brutal as you like. And I very much want you to tell me if all the Agatha Christie bits of it work or not because I'm not very good at clues and red herrings and things like that ...'

'I'm terribly sorry but I've got to ring off. That was the front door bell and it may be something important so I'd better answer it,' I said. This emergency – often fallaciously invoked in the past to provide an excuse for abruptly ending a draining talk on the telephone which threatened to go on until some definite plan for a meeting had been arranged – was for once an actuality. I was prepared for Harriet (seldom fooled) to counter it by a callous 'Let it ring: I haven't finished' but instead she replied with satisfaction: 'I know what it is – that'll be the mini-cab I sent the manuscript round in. They *have* been quick! Do hurry down and open the door ... Oh darling I told the man he'd be paid your end, you don't mind, do you?'

But it wasn't the mini-cab at the door: it was Jeremy, nearly obliterated by a vast fur coat which had recently been bequeathed to him by an aunt. This tubular sheath of yellowish curls, punctuated by pale patches of baldness, stretched from a collar concealing his ears to the hem of its skirt round his ankles. From a pocket in its folds, somewhere near his heart, he produced some typewritten pages of lined foolscap fastened together by a small gold safety-pin. As if hypnotised, I accepted them from his hand, feeling like the last, doomed player in a game of Old Maid. 'Won't stay,' he whispered. 'Can't come in. This is for you. To read, if you can face it. It's *tremendously* important to me what you think of it. I won't say more – only that somebody's whole future as a creative artist depends on your opinion. One more thing, and then I'll leave you in peace: if you *love* it, ring me tonight. And if you *hate* it – lie. Because that's something I just wouldn't be able to take. Bless you. Take care.' He blew me a middle- and forefinger kiss; then, his body bent in a purposeful stride and occasionally stumbling over the coat, he hurried off down the street just as Hurricane Harriet's mini-cab drew up at the kerb where he had been standing.

Yes, something had to be done.

And then I had an idea.

It first came to me one pale summer evening about two months after the memorial service. I was wandering down Westbourne Grove, headed for home past the local landmarks with their intense but limited associations: John Nodes, Funerals; austere, exotic Baba Bhelpoori; the convent, mysterious in its quiet seclusion, of the Bon Secours Nursing Sisters; the block of mansion flats where (as Jeremy once told me – it was the kind of thing he knew) Irene Handl lived; Elliott the shoe shop on the corner with that maddening squiggle under the tiny, crooked, elevated golden 'o'. As I approached my own front door I heard the sound, both plaintive as a mew and contented as a purr, of a telephone ringing not so very far away and (assuming it to be my own) walked straight on without pausing or turning my head, as if it were necessary to mislead some phantom follower by pretending that the house had nothing to do with me. If I had entered the flat, and my telephone *had* been ringing, I should have answered it – although (as I often reminded myself) there was no necessity to do so as neither Jeremy nor Harriet could possibly know that I was in. It was in order to forestall this weakness that I had refrained from going indoors, suddenly realising that there was no necessity to do that either.

On the other hand, I had to be somewhere ... I turned into Micky's Fish Bar, sat at a table and began to read the label on what looked like a bottle of vinegar. 'Sheik non-brewed condiment', it said. 'Unexcelled for its purity and keeping properties. Ingredients: acetic acid and caramel ...' I ordered a vanilla ice from the Italian waiter and I thought: 'What am I doing in this pointless place, as if I had no home of my own to go to? Why am I behaving like someone in flight? How is it that I have come to feel so pathetically at the mercy of these two benevolent and affectionate creatures? Why do I allow them to hound me? I could just tell them to leave me alone. But that would hurt them. Is that what I'm afraid of, then – hurting people? Evidently. Is there *no* reason I might give for not wanting to see so much of them that would spare their feelings and also have some effect? Well, there is *one* excuse for neglecting one's friends (other than work, which seems to have failed in this case) which is always accepted with equanimity and even respect. A love affair! Exactly. Both Jeremy and Harriet would only be happily reconciled to scarcely seeing me at all if they believed that the time I spent out of their company was sacrificed to the demands of some over-riding sexual and romantic passion. It's true that I am not involved at the moment in any such relationship, but that's no snag, for surely nothing could be simpler than to pretend that I am. If I don't find a lover, I shall just have to invent one.'

As things turned out, it became necessary to invent two.

After arriving at my decision, I was nervously undecided about what means to choose of putting it into effect; Harriet's first call, however, could be said to have played straight into my hands. She had herself just embarked on a flirtation with a successful author of science fiction and was anxious to take it a stage further, but was finding it difficult to deceive her resident boy friend. Would I provide her with an alibi? 'Of course he won't check up, but just in case he should, remember – I was with you all tomorrow evening.' I said I would be delighted to oblige, and muttered something fairly incoherent about being in the same sort of situation myself. She sounded rather surprised. 'Oh, really? Somehow or other I didn't think of you as going in for scenes.' But she did not on that occasion ask any questions: her own adventure was naturally monopolising her attention. Relieved at having so effortlessly broken the ice, I felt confident of coping with Jeremy's next approach.

This took an unexpected form. 'I'm making my will,' he announced, 'and I can't tell you what fun it is. Have you made yours recently? You must... Anyway, I'm putting you down as one of my literary executors and I'm going to leave you a tiny something as well though I haven't yet quite made up my mind what it will be. Would you prefer a little cash, or some personal belonging of mine, like a book? Think about it and let me know – there's no hurry. I know you'll make a marvellous literary executor. I hope you don't mind my asking – if you find the idea too much of a bore, just say so – but I think you'll have quite an interesting time going through all my letters and so on and deciding what ought to be done with them. And by the way, if you *do* feel like bringing your own will up to date, I would simply love to return the compliment and be *your* literary executor. There's always such a muddle when somebody dies, and it might be a relief to know that a friend you can absolutely trust would come flying round at once and destroy anything you didn't want kept. I think you can rely on me to understand your wishes and respect them.' In momentary confusion, I was about to ask how he would be able to dash round and inspect my private papers when he was already dead himself, but instead I explained that I was rather preoccupied at that moment with an affair of the heart, and found it hard to concentrate on anything else. This was greeted by a very long pause. At length Jeremy said: 'Wow! Well, all I can say, my dear, is congratters! I think that's a simply fantastic piece of news. The moment you feel like telling me more about it I shall be all ears. And needless to say, should you ever want any advice . . . But I'll take the hint and leave you in peace for the time being.' He hung up, and that was that.

Subsequent, less guarded conversations made one thing clear: Jeremy and Harriet had formed startlingly opposite views about the nature of my sexual partner. As I had never made any kind of pass at either of them, Harriet had convinced herself that I was gay while Jeremy had vaguely assumed that I must be straight. When they began to inquire a little further about the course of my romance, she automatically used the masculine pronoun and he the feminine. Somehow unable to maintain a total silence on the subject, I found myself gradually divulging small items of information about my imaginary lover, subtly attuned to fit in with the preconceptions of my two listeners. Thus the lover split into twin images, male and female, Apollo and Venus, Yin and Yang, and from a series of hints and denials while talking on the telephone two separate personalities were brought into being: that of Linda and that of Tone.

Tone, of course, was short for Tony, who originally acquired his name as a result of Harriet mis-hearing a remark of mine quite unconnected with the subject. The Electric Cinema was showing a Pasolini season and I must have volunteered something like 'I'm going to *Accatone* tonight', which she interpreted as 'I'm going back to Tony tonight', assuming that I had quarrelled with my friend but had decided on a reconciliation. Emboldened by this breakthrough, Harriet soon after it risked a leading question: 'What does Tony *do*?' My mind at that moment was almost blank; I happened to be staring at a newspaper headline containing the fashionable acronym 'Quango' which (as I wasn't wearing my reading spectacles) I misread as 'Qantas'; I answered, before I had properly taken thought, 'He works as an airline steward.' He was thus established as an Australian, and the diminutive 'Tone' seemed naturally to follow.

Linda's primary characteristics were more slow in taking shape because Jeremy, though just as inquisitive as Harriet, chose less direct methods of satisfying his curiosity. It was not long, however, before a few tentative facts emerged: she was an actress, though not yet well known; she had been named after Linda Darnell, her mother's favourite film star; she adored cats, but was allergic to their fur. She was involved with various liberal causes, and sometimes asked me to accompany her on protest marches. (Tone, on the other hand, while claiming to be totally non-political, would often express opinions that were uncomfortably close to Fascism.) When I first met her Linda had been a passionate admirer of the works of Tolkien but (possibly under my influence) was now beginning to grow out of them.

Such feeble scraps of elementary data were about all that Jeremy and Harriet managed to glean from me, but the knowledge that at any time I might be called upon to produce fuller details of personal description kept my imagination perpetually on the alert, and I gradually amassed substantial dossiers on both Linda and Tone, to be held in readiness at the back of my brain in case of sudden need. My ruse, though succeeding in one sense more completely than I had anticipated, must therefore be said to have failed in its ultimate purpose – to win more time for myself in which to work on the memoir: I had gained the time, but only to fritter it away in maddening, monotonous, obsessive speculation about these two irrelevant inventions. The reserves of energy which, liberated from the exorbitant demands of friendship, should have flowed into the mainstream of literary creation, found themselves disastrously diverted into a sterile tributary, from the imprisoning banks of which there was no apparent release.

But it wasn't until last Tuesday that things began to get downright funny. I'd come home from work and was sitting on the sofa surrounded by comfortable stubby pencils and sturdy yellow pads but hadn't yet made any notes. Guiltily, I thought I'd have a look at the *Guardian* crossword, but when I folded the paper at the right page I found it had already been filled in by somebody else. This seemed decidedly spooky; until, after a minute, I remembered that, of *course*, I had done the whole puzzle myself while having my morning coffee. That shook me, rather. Was I completely losing my memory? Or just not taking things in? Then the telephone rang. I knew it couldn't be Jeremy, because he believed that I always spent Tuesdays with Linda (he had a catch-phrase: 'Tuesday night is lover night') and I had instructed him never to disturb me on that evening. So it could only be Hurricane Harriet. I didn't lift the receiver immediately, but a dogged quality in the ring told me that she wasn't going to give up easily (why is it that some people ring on and on as if they knew you were there while others hang up almost at once so that you couldn't answer even if you wanted to?) and eventually I succumbed.

'Hi. Listen. I hope I'm not interrupting anything but I've just *got* to tell you something, that's all. You'll be simply fascinated. You'll never guess what it is, never in a million years. Are you ready? Well, here goes – I've met Tone!'

Needless to say, I was much more surprised by this announcement than she could have possibly expected, but I tried to betray no greater degree of amazement than might strike her as normal. 'Are you sure?' I asked cautiously.

'*Almost* sure – no, I *am* sure, I'm quite certain it was him. For God's sake don't worry, I was terribly discreet and never mentioned your name or anything like that. So he's absolutely no idea that I know you or have ever heard about him.'

'Well, I'm glad of that. But when did you meet him? And where?'

'Last night. I'd been invited to drinks by a girl I used to know years ago and of course had no intention of going but then at about six o'clock I suddenly got fed up with thinking I'd got agoraphobia and decided the thing to do was get *out* of the house by hook or by crook so I rang up an Austin Princess and took it to Hampstead and told it to wait outside for twenty minutes while I went to this creepy party. Of course the whole thing turned out to be a total failure and the party was a *complete* nightmare, but never mind, I was introduced to this young man who when he opened his mouth sounded like that Barry

Humphries character, you know, the Cultural Attaché to the Court of St James's, so I knew he was Australian for a start, and when I asked him what he did he said he was a Qantas airline steward, and when I asked his name he said it was Tony Something or other, now isn't that too extraordinary for words? ... Actually, darling, you never told me how wildly attractive he is.'

'Perhaps I didn't like to boast,' I heard myself coyly saying.

'You sound awfully self-conscious, and I must say I *quite* see why. I suppose I'm being frightfully embarrassing – I *am* sorry – but I can't help it.'

'I'm not in the least embarrassed. It's just that I'm not yet quite convinced. There must be *hundreds* of Qantas airline stewards. Well, maybe not hundreds – but lots, anyhow,' I finished lamely.

'But how many of them are called Tony?' Harriet persisted. 'I tell you, that *was* him I spoke to yesterday. I just know it, and that's all there is to it. But I'll never breathe another word about it as long as I live if you'd really rather I didn't.'

'It might be better – just for the time being – if we *didn't* discuss it any more,' I said. 'There's a sort of reason for keeping it all a secret which I can't quite explain – that's all part of why it has to *be* a secret, if you see what I mean.'

'I don't see what you mean at all, love. Not in this day and age, I don't, with everybody leaping out of the closet left right and centre like so many *kangaroos*. To tell you the truth, I think it's a little bit snobbish of you to be ashamed of Tone. I thought he was *sweet*.'

'I'm not in the least ashamed of Tone,' I

defended myself at random. 'In fact, it would be much nearer the point to say that *he's* ashamed of *me*. But that's all part of this tiresome business which I really mustn't talk about at this stage.'

'Is it because he's married, or something?'

'I *told* you, I don't wish to talk about it,' I said with exasperated dignity – and then spoilt the effect by asking: 'Why, did he mention being married?'

'No, of course not. We hardly spoke two words to each other, if you must know. Oh well, I'm sorry if I've been tactless. I just thought you'd be interested, that's all. It's no skin off *my* nose whether you ever utter his name again. It's nothing on earth to do with *me*.'

'I was fascinated by what you said. Thank you for telling me.'

'OK, darling. See you later.' Hurricane rang off.

This ludicrous conversation, innocent enough when you analyse it, left me with a feeling of irritation which quite prevented me from doing any work that night, and even made it impossible for me to concentrate on a book or television. On the following evening I still felt vaguely upset by it, and began to wonder whether there was any point in what I was trying to write, or indeed in anyone writing anything at all – a dangerous frame of mind. So I was almost relieved when the telephone rang, and not too depressed to hear Jeremy's voice on the other end of the line.

'Is this a bad moment?' he asked.

'Not a bit.'

'I know it's not lover night, but you're sure

you're not watching telly or just having a lovely meditation or anything?'

'No, this is fine.'

'Well, are you sitting down? Have you got a drink in your hand? You're going to need it. Because I've got great news! Great, great news ... And I'm not going to spoil it by telling you what it is straight away. You've got to guess. God, I am enjoying this! Now, guess, who do you think I met today? I'll give you a clue – no, I won't. I'll give you three questions and then you've got to guess. Only three. Go on. Fire away.'

'Man or woman?'

'Woman.'

'Where did you meet her?'

'Lunchtime theatre – the Soho Poly. I was in the audience and so was she.'

'Linda?'

'Right! Brilliant! Well? I knew you'd be riveted.'

'How do you know it was Linda? I mean, *my* Linda?'

'I sort of felt it in my bones. The boy I was with introduced us – Linda Something, he said, I can't remember the last name. And when I asked her what she did she said she was on the stage, mainly fringe things, lunchtime and so on. I thought she was *fantastically* nice and sympathetic, I really fell madly in love with her in a way and I couldn't understand more what you see in her ... but I'm being insensitive, aren't I? I'll shut up in a minute, I promise. But I just had to tell you because it was all so odd. I can't get over it, actually, I mean if one put it in a story nobody would believe it, my bumping into her like that when I'm the *only* person who knows about you and her . . . That's all I wanted to say. I'll ring off now. *Lots* of love. You don't mind, do you? See you very soon. 'Bye,' he ended in a soft gasp.

Poor Jeremy had meant no harm, but this exchange left me with a sense of outrage. The pompous phrase 'invasion of privacy' entered my mind and lingered there, somehow comforting in its overtone of righteous indignation. The whole situation seemed to be getting out of hand! All right, so I had lied – but there was no malice in my falsehood; rather it had been nearer (or so I hoped) to that exercise of the imagination necessary for art. Now I understood what my punishment was: to be believed. My powers of invention were called into question; I had been taken literally; irresponsible fantasy was reduced to inconvenient fact. I felt angry, as though I had been caught out in something shameful, and sad, as though I had suffered yet another deprivation, and frightened, as though I had lost my way in hitherto familiar terrain. 'Wait till tomorrow,' I told myself. 'You'll have forgotten about it by then.'

Thursday evening: I still couldn't work. There are two kinds of writer's block. With one, you know what you want to say but find it impossible to choose between the alternative ways of expressing your thought: there seem to be too many words at your disposal. With the other, your mind goes hollow and the very word 'idea' becomes a meaningless concept, while your vocabulary shrinks to a few stale tokens. I had the second kind of block.

I switched on the television. Before the picture came into focus, I could hear a voice say good-humouredly: 'You've about as much charm as a dyspeptic alligator' and the dutiful laugh of a studio audience. Then the screen showed a group of people playing a word game called 'Blankety Blank'. Terry Wogan continued his pretence of insulting a guest celebrity. 'Haven't I spoken to you before about not answering back?' he was saying when my telephone rang. I stretched out my toe to extinguish the programme while I stretched out my hand to lift the receiver. Would it be Jeremy this time, or was it the turn of Hurricane Harriet? Indifference prevented me from saying 'hullo' and during the second or so of silence that ensued I suddenly guessed who it was at the other end of the line. When the caller spoke – 'Hi. Are you there?' – the marked accent convinced me that my intuition had been correct. You could say that I recognised the voice, although in fact I was hearing it for the first time. 'Yes, I'm here,' I replied.

'Sorry to call you up out of the blue like this, but I thought maybe it was time for us two to get together.'

'Yes, I think it is. High time.'

'Sure you don't mind?' said Tone. 'I mean, is it really all right, me calling?'

'No, I'm very glad that you did.'

'Then what about meeting up for a jar one evening? How does that strike you?'

'I think it's a very good idea. When do you suggest?'

'How are you fixed tomorrow, say around six?'

'That would be perfect. Where shall we meet?'

'Think you can find your way to Chiswick?'

'Of course.'

'There's a pub down there, just around the corner from the Qantas Regional Headquarters Admin Building, where me and some of the guys do some of our drinking some of the time. They get a nice crowd there. Nothing flash, but a friendly atmosphere. I use it quite a lot because it's handy for the orifice – I *beg* your pardon, I will read that again – handy for the office. It's called "The Ground Hostess". Think you can find it?'

'I'll manage.'

'Don't be late, will you, there's a good bloke?'

'I'm never late.'

'See you tomorrow, then.'

'Right.'

I think that was all that we said. After I had hung up I immediately opened my engagement book and wrote down '6.00 p.m. The Ground Hostess' on the page for Friday: this act made the recent telephone conversation seem more real. Then I tried to imagine telling another person about what had just happened. They – he – she – whoever it was that I confided in – would almost certainly suggest that somebody had been playing a practical joke on me. This explanation of the mystery struck me as unlikely. Harriet could never have disguised her voice to sound like the man who had rung me up. It is true that Jeremy just conceivably might have done so – but then he knew nothing at all about the existence of Tone. Not that 'existence' was exactly the *mot juste* . . . or was it? I was reminded of a short story by Anatole France, which made a deep impression on me when I read it a long time ago. It's about a woman who invents a fictitious character called Putois as an excuse for getting out of any boring social engagement, and this figment of her imagination gradually assumes a life of its own. I think the story may have been at the back of my mind when I first embarked on the stratagem of Linda and Tone. Anyway, as far as I can remember it ends with the woman being told that a Monsieur Putois had called to see her while she was out . . . I decided that the best thing to do for the time being was to think about nothing: blankety blank. Then the telephone rang again. I picked up the receiver and said at once: 'Is that you, Linda?'

She sounded slightly taken aback. Like Tone, she began by apologising: was I quite sure that I didn't mind her ringing up like this, 'out of the blue'? I agreed with her that it was high time we got to know each other. In my conversation with Tone, the initiative had remained with him throughout; but with Linda, I was able to take it out of her hands from the start. I told her that I would be having a drink at 'The Ground Hostess' at six o'clock on the following day, and invited her to join me there. She didn't know the pub, but thought she could find it without much difficulty. Yes, she'd love to come, she said. Something hesitant in her voice made me think that she needed reassurance, and with a rather ridiculous approach to old-world courtesy I told her how much I looked forward to making her acquaintance.

'And I'm *dying* to make *yours*.'
'See you tomorrow, then.'
'Right.'

After this, I left the telephone receiver off the hook. I swallowed my last two Mogadons and passed a long night of dreamless sleep. Looking back on it now, I'm not quite sure how I spent the early part of the next day. At one stage I must have rung the office with some excuse for staying at home: I was much too excited to go to work. And then I know that I searched everywhere for my copy of Kafka containing his 'Reflections on Sin, Pain, Hope and the True Way' because I needed to remind myself of the last page, and that I finally found it on the edge of a shelf about lunchtime. 'You do not need to leave your room. Remain sitting at your table and listen. Do not even listen, simply wait. Do not even wait, be quite still and solitary. The world will freely offer itself to you to be unmasked, it has no choice, it will roll in ecstasy at your feet.'

Yes, that's what I wanted to read again. I even typed it out on my Hermes Baby in the hope of ramming its message home. But it wasn't any good. I still had to get to Chiswick to keep the appointments I had made. Then I needed my A to Z *London Street Atlas* and that took a bit of finding too – though not so long as the Kafka. I worked out a route, and set off in plenty of time. At the Notting Hill tube, where I usually boarded a train on the Central line to carry me east to work, I took one instead on the District line travelling west. This subtle adjustment of a daily routine had about it something aberrant, as in a dream where perverse and disturbing events occur among natural and familiar surroundings.

Incurably afraid of being late, I reached the meeting-place at twenty past five, and had to wait outside for ten fretful minutes. I felt something of the desperate impatience of an alcoholic as I counted the seconds till opening time. Ignoring my surroundings in the street, I stared at the locked, chained and bolted door: the world of my imagination had shrunk to whatever lay beyond it. When at last I heard and saw signs of its being opened, I felt that this predictable event had only been brought about by the intensity of my concentration.

For some reason I waited a further, unnecessary moment or two before entering the pub. The pale youth who had admitted me had now gone behind the bar and was talking in an undertone to his colleague, a middle-aged woman with dyed red hair. Neither of them took any notice of me. The room, which was otherwise empty, struck me as abnormally large. The bar occupied the centre, and the surrounding space had presumably once been divided into partitions – saloon, public, private, snuggery and so on. The removal of these had left behind an impression of desolate immensity. The walls were papered in a timid design, pale brown on cream, faintly reminiscent of the jazz patterns admired in the 1920s, and this fussy motif was repeated on the plastic seats of the banquettes. What little colour the decor contained (paintings of Spanish dancers on the walls; dark green tin ashtrays on the tables; the domesticated rainbow effect, like an old-fashioned chemist's shop-window, of the bottles behind the bar) seemed to be suddenly sucked away when the barmaid switched on the overhead strip lighting. At the same moment, the youth tuned in to a radio. Frank Sinatra and his daughter were singing an old number: 'And then I go and spoil it all by saying something stupid like – I love you.'

I bought a Bloody Mary and took it over to a corner. A limp evening paper had been left behind by one of the morning customers. As it was a *Racing Standard*, most of it was already out of date, but I glanced at Katina (never at her best on a Friday, when she had to provide a comprehensive forecast for the weekend and Monday) and read the whole of Bridge with Rixi. I had just started Classics on Cassette by Christopher Grier when I was overwhelmed by a feeling of restlessness and began to wander round the room. I still had nearly half an hour in which to explore 'The Ground Hostess'.

There was more to see than I had realised at first. A blank television screen hung from the ceiling, tilted forward at a tipsy angle. The lavatory doors were identified by twin ideograms, one tubular and one triangular, suggestive of trousers and skirt. A wide, shining jukebox: this I was tempted to play, but its music would have conflicted with the barman's radio and I lacked the courage to risk anything approaching provocation. A form of football for two players, featuring a quivering dot of electric light, like Tinker Bell in *Peter Pan*, and accompanied by a thin, non-stop, whining noise. A more than usually complicated fruit machine, offering an extreme variety of winning permutations and bewildering instructions: 'Reel may be nudged in chosen direction by selecting nudge up or nudge down when nudge panels flash. Nudges available as lit. During a game numbers on win line light letters of word NUDGE. Players may hold numbers to complete word and achieve Nudge Feature.' This, however, was out of order. A game called Master Mind, which tests your IQ and rates the result in categories ranging from Average to Genius. It asked me who wrote *Paradise Lost* – John Milton, John Osborne, Shakespeare or Margaret Mitchell? I pressed the button for Milton, but the machine firmly indicated that my answer was incorrect. I think it must have been out of order too.

Then I visited the Gents, although I had no desire to piss. There were some puzzling graffiti: 'I thought pubic hair was a friend of Bugs Bunny until I discovered Smirnoff'; 'My girl's so dumb she thinks Hertz Van Rental is a Dutch footballer'; 'Who is Milton Keynes? An economist. No, that's Maynard Keynes. No, that's Milton Friedman. Both wrong – he's a sadistic poet.' This place seemed to have an obsession with Milton: did he (I found myself bemusedly almost wondering) have any connection with Chiswick? Pulling myself together, I went back to the remains of my drink and the *Racing Standard*, in which I located the TV Guide on an unfamiliar page with a new photograph of Celia Brayfield. A young couple came into the pub, walking very close to each other. It was only when I noticed that they were holding white sticks that I understood that they were blind. They stood talking together happily for a while (I heard the man say: 'She's Steering Wheel – you know, the Motoring Correspondent for *Hullabaloo*') and then he deliberately approached the bar and negotiated the purchase of two drinks. He returned to the girl and they sat, just touching, in companionable silence.

The red-haired woman behind the bar was more audible now. 'Do you the world of good,' she was saying. 'Take you out of yourself. You don't want to sit on your bum for the rest of your life feeling sorry for yourself, now, do you? Oh, if I was you, I wouldn't think twice. You wouldn't see me for dust. Leap at the chance, that's what I'd do. I know what I'm talking about. I've been there, haven't I? Oh, when it comes to that, I wrote the book ...'

'That's all very well,' said the pale-faced youth. 'It's easy to talk like that. But I don't know, I'm sure ... Dashing around like a fart in a bubble-bath – where does it get you? You only have to come home in the end, when all's said and done.'

I had become so engrossed in this dialogue that I had forgotten my purpose in coming to the pub. I felt panic. Where was I? Who was I? I looked at my watch, as if the answer to these questions lay there. It was six o'clock. I raised the newspaper to cover the lower part of my face, and over its top I gazed at the entrance to the street. The door opened, and Tone came in.

He was shorter than I had expected; indeed, his figure could almost be described as stocky. His hair was concealed by a furry Russian hat, his eyes by large rimless glasses and his mouth by a soft brown moustache of the kind once known as

'Zapata'. He wore a navy blue jacket with a double vent and bright brass buttons; a fawn polo-neck pullover of thin wool which wrinkled so tightly over his chest that his nipples were visible in outline beneath it; conventional blue jeans; and lace-up canvas kicker boots of vivid orange and chalky white. Over one arm he carried a neatly folded raincoat, also navy blue, and under the other he held a smart black briefcase. He looked round the room in a manner both cautious and arrogant, but seemed to find nothing in it to arrest his attention; then he crossed to the bar with a jaunty strut that betrayed to me his lack of social confidence. After carefully placing his briefcase and raincoat on one stool he hoisted himself on to another, leaned his elbows on the counter, cupped his face with his hands and stared fixedly in front of him. When the barmaid moved into his line of vision, he spoke. 'Lager and lime, please, dear, if it's not too much trouble.' After paying for the drink he resumed this semi-crouching posture, from which it was difficult to tell if his mood was meditative, sulky or shy. Every so often he shot out his wrist and consulted an expensive-looking digital watch. There was something faintly sinister about him, like a character in a book by Frederick Forsyth, and at the same time something so sharply poignant that I ached with pity at the memory of his shallow vulnerability and shivered at my intimate knowledge of his deserved discomforts.

Anyway, it was quite clear that he hadn't taken *me* in. I began to wonder what on earth I was doing, sitting here in this really rather depressing place. I was about to get up and go over to talk to him (though I had not yet rehearsed any opening remark) when the door opened once again. How typical of Linda, I thought, to time her arrival exactly ten minutes after the agreed hour. Women are always self-conscious about entering pubs alone, so she could not have risked being the first to get there; at the same time, she had enough consideration for others not to be annoyingly late.

She wore jeans, plimsolls and a child's Snoopy T-shirt. She was pale and slight, her fragile figure scarcely able to support the weight of her immense leather shoulder-bag, which was heavily tasselled and embroidered with a design of vaguely peasant origin. Her dark hair was cropped short, giving an effect of careless austerity which only emphasised the beauty of her violet eyes, straight thin nose and short upper lip, helplessly lifted over tiny china teeth. She was clearly nervous, for she hovered on the threshold of the room as if she still might escape back into the street; it looked as if she could not bring herself to shut the door behind her. 'Make up your mind, darling, if you don't mind,' the barmaid called out. 'That's one hell of a draught you're creating by just standing there.' 'Sorry,' said Linda, and she let the door bang to, imprisoning herself in the pub. She gazed searchingly at the sightless couple, as though appealing for some kind of help which of course they were unable to provide, and then carefully examined the rest of the room. I had once more defensively lifted the newspaper but above it my eyes met hers for a moment, and I can only say, in the words of the cliché, that she seemed to 'look straight through me'. For a while she studied Tone's back view with no expression on her face, and then deliberately walked to a part of the bar some distance from his seat but where he would be able to see her if he ever raised his eyes from his drink, into which he was now intently staring. She ordered a Tio Pepe, and after it was bought consumed it with delicate sips, evenly spaced, as if performing a ritual. She gave an impression of innocent refinement and seemed lost in some private reverie – 'miles away', as they say – but I knew that in fact she was acutely conscious of everything that took place around her and I ached with pity at the memory of her proud little gaucheries and shivered at my intimate knowledge of her touchingly hard-earned triumphs.

Tone finished his lager and lime with a deep draught, smacked his lips, made an appreciative noise and ordered a large Scotch. While it was being fetched he added: 'And kindly be so good as to give the young lady opposite another glass of whatever it is she's having.' Linda began to protest, but Tone raised his hands and insistently pushed their palms in her direction several times. 'My pleasure, my pleasure,' he repeated. Linda soon gave in, and when she was halfway through her second sherry Tone gathered his belongings together and ceremoniously carried them over to a stool next to hers. He offered her a Marlboro, and while she was fumbling in her cavernous shoulder-bag for a box of matches he efficiently clicked a pale blue Crickette lighter to which she submissively dipped her head.

There were now three groups in 'The Ground

Hostess' carrying on conversations too low for me to overhear: the blind pair, the two behind the bar, and Linda and Tone. But I didn't need to know what they were saying – I had heard it all before. 'Oh, when it comes to that, I wrote the book . . .' After a few more minutes Tone was handing Linda down off her stool and escorting her to the door. He turned and with uneasy affability said ''Night, all' to the room at large; then they left the pub together. There's no doubt that they made a very attractive couple, and as I watched them vanish I couldn't help feeling a twinge of pride at the thought that if it hadn't been for me they might never have met.